'You're marrie~~~anger clearing~~~

He held her hand up in ~~~ ~~~ put his index finger on the gold band on her ring finger.

She smiled brightly, and drew him closer. 'Yes. Isn't it wonderful?'

'Christy! What in hell are you doing in my bed?' He pushed her away, trying to sort through details he couldn't seem to bring together.

She grinned wickedly. That was an expression she'd never had in the old days. 'How can you have been so magnificent and not remember?'

He put his hand to the pain in his forehead. It wasn't like him not to remember a sexual encounter. 'I don't know what happened. I don't remember. But you're married and I don't play around with married women.'

'Paul, it's all right.' She knelt on the mattress and reached out to catch his left hand. A gold band that matched the one on her third finger winked in the sunlight. 'I'm married to *you*.'

Dear Reader,

This month we're pleased to welcome new-to-Silhouette® author Angela Benson. Her debut book for Special Edition®, *A Family Wedding*, is a warm, wonderful tale of friends falling in love...and a darling little girl's dream come true.

We're also proud to present Victoria Pade's fun tale, *Mum for Hire*, our THAT'S MY BABY! title. Bailey Coltrain wants to be a mum, so she thinks she should get some experience first—with the hero's kids! And please welcome to Special Edition, veteran Silhouette Desire® author Peggy Moreland, by reading *Rugrats and Rawhide* —a tender tale of unexpected fatherhood.

Sherryl Woods returns with a marvellous new series—THE BRIDAL PATH. Don't miss the first book, *A Ranch for Sara*, a rollicking heart-warming love story. The second and third titles will be available in September and October. And the thermostat continues to rise with Gina Wilkins's sparkling tale of opposites attracting in *The Father Next Door*.

Finally, Muriel Jensen presents readers with the perfect revenge title—*The Wedding Gamble*. This tale of love lost and then rediscovered is full of life.

We hope you enjoy this book, and each and every title to come!

The Editors

The Wedding Gamble
MURIEL JENSEN

SILHOUETTE

SPECIAL EDITION ®

*Silhouette, Silhouette Special Edition and Colophon are
registered trademarks of Harlequin Books S.A., used under licence.*

*First published in Great Britain 1997
Silhouette Books, Eton House, 18-24 Paradise Road,
Richmond, Surrey TW9 1SR*

© Muriel Jensen 1994

ISBN 0 373 16549 8

23-9708

*Printed and bound in Great Britain
by Mackays of Chatham PLC, Chatham*

Other novels by Muriel Jensen

Silhouette Sensation®

Love and Lavender
Fantasies and Memories
The Duck Shack Agreement
Strings
Side by Side
A Carol Christmas
The Miracle
Valentine Hearts and Flowers

Prologue

Paul Bertrand sat on a bench in Soldier's Green and looked around him at the colonial and contemporary architecture that identified downtown Eternity, Massachusetts. Thomas Wolfe's famous quote "You can't go home again" crossed his mind, and the hardened investigative reporter in him rebelled at the triteness of the thought. He preferred to think that he was simply back where he'd been born, back where he grew up and graduated from high school. Eternity had ceased to be home when his mother left.

Boston was where he belonged. It was a city that knew how to mingle cobblestones and concrete and still function. It lived with a foot in the past and an eye to the future. It wasn't stuck in its history or awash in sentimentality as Eternity seemed to be...as *he* seemed to be.

Paul stood, impatient with himself and all the warm memories washing over him. He'd once stood in this very square with his friends and considered a Saturday afternoon's options in entertainment. There'd been movies, bowling, boating or their favorite pastime—daring each other to go deeper and deeper into the old abandoned lace factory on the Sussex River.

A thoughtful smile pulled at his lips as he remembered how big they'd felt, battling cobwebs, walking farther into the building despite things that moved in the shadows, and ignoring the tales they'd heard of unearthly happenings, tales that had been passed down generations of adventurous boys.

The smile left as quickly as it had come. His mother had moved away from Eternity, leaving him behind and he hadn't felt big at all. He'd felt small and lost until he'd figured out where to direct the blame.

But he'd deal with his father later. Right now he had something else to do, someone else to see. He had a wrong to right that had gnawed at his gut all the years he'd been building a reputation as a journalistic power at the *Boston Globe.*

He had to find Christy and tell her he was sorry.

He loped across First Street and waited on the corner of Bridge for the light afternoon traffic to pass. He glanced at the eighteenth-century stone bridge on his left, remembering vividly what it had been like to be a teenager in love. He stopped to indulge himself for a minute. This wasn't just nostalgia, this was at the heart of who he was—a man who'd been infatuated with a plain and very earnest young woman because everything had seemed so clear to her, and he'd felt so confused.

He'd kissed her for the first time on that bridge after they'd taken the school newspaper to the printer' one cold November night. They'd uncovered a scandal, as he recalled—something about the speech contest being fixed so that Molly Beausoleil won. He didn't remember the particulars, only that they'd felt like Woodward and Bernstein, and a friendship that had been building for the two years they'd worked on the *Eagle* took a turn that night that startled both of them.

On the night of the senior prom, they'd stood on this bridge and he'd asked her to marry him. Then he'd come to the same spot the night before the wedding and faced the fact that he couldn't go through with it—and that he didn't have the guts to tell her. Instead, he'd picked up his bag and gotten on the bus to Boston.

Hands in the pockets of his slacks, he turned in the direction of the shop his cousin had told him he'd find at the west end of First Street.

He'd never adjusted to the guilt. It lived always in a little corner of his being, throwing a slight pall over all his achievements. And sometimes he lay awake at night and imagined Christy, gangly and plain, blue eyes filled with pain at his cowardly abandonment.

He drew a bracing breath and remembered Jacqui's directions. "There are a bunch of little shops in a row with lavender awnings, all part of the Weddings, Inc. group. You can't miss it."

But Jacqui had failed to mention what kind of a shop Christy owned. He looked at the logos on the awnings and identified a print shop, a dress shop, a hair salon, and a place called Honeymoon Hideaway. He headed for the print shop, thinking that related most closely to Christy's old lust for the newspaper business, then the fine print on one of the awnings caught his attention.

He stared at it. Honeymoon Hideaway, Christine Bowman, Prop. He frowned and wandered slowly toward the next shop. In the artfully decorated window were massage oils, edible undies, bath gels with erotic labels, nearly nothing bikinis, and a maid's outfit that was transparent and could be measured in inches.

Interspersed among the sensual items were practical things. Aspirin, film, travel journals, paperbacks, suntan lotion. In a corner of the window was a sign that promised *Every*thing You Need for Your Honeymoon.

Paul stepped back again to make sure he hadn't misread the sign. He hadn't. He stared at it in perplexity. Proper, earnest Christine Bowman sold edible panties?

Then two young women walked out of the shop, giggling, and as the door closed slowly, he heard the sound of laughter from inside—Christy's laughter.

Paul dug his sunglasses out of the pocket of his tweed jacket and put them on. Then he shouldered his way into the shop.

He saw her immediately. Three young men were clustered around her, towering over her, yet apparently completely under her spell. He knew she was Christy because he heard her laugh again. The sound was low and musical, and when he'd been eighteen, it used to make his body temperature rise ten degrees.

He was surprised to find that hadn't changed. But Christy had. As she explained to her rapt audience the muscle-relaxing properties of the contents of the bottle she held in her hand, he stared—looking for some sign, any sign, of the slender, ponytailed girl he used to know.

This young woman wore a gray wool dress that rested off her shoulders, revealing elegant white skin. The wool clung to her shapely breasts, tiny waist and neat hips, and ended several inches above her knees.

Her hair, a side-parted cloud of dark brown that she had to keep tossing back from her eye, fell well past her shoulders in gleaming ripples. The woman who had once shunned makeup as too time-consuming to apply now had long, dark eyelashes, cheekbones that shimmered mauve under the practical fluorescent lighting and lips that were full and luscious.

The overall effect was gorgeous—but completely unsettling.

The little group moved apart as she rounded the counter on spindly black heels to ring up the sale. What the action did to the hips under the wool made him feel strangled. He slipped behind a tall display of paperbacks, breathing deeply to fight off asphyxiation and annoyance.

He told himself he was irritated because he didn't want to be in Eternity. But his father had broken his leg and had called for his help, and there was little else he could do without appearing to be a cold, uncaring boor. He'd decided to come and settle up with Louis once and for all.

No. This didn't have to do with his father. This had to do with Christy and the fact that he'd held this image in his mind of a lonely, heartbroken young woman struggling to cope without him because no one would ever understand her the way he had.

He was looking at proof that he'd been very, very mistaken.

The young man who now held the lavender-and-white sack containing his purchase leaned an elbow on the counter and leered at Christy. "Now just where," he asked quietly, obviously out to get a reaction, "do I put this stuff on her?" The young men with him exchanged grinning looks.

"It's a muscle-easing oil," she replied, her eyebrow raised at his flirtatious tone. "If you're not sure what to do with it, give it to her and let her use it on you. I'm sure she'll figure it out."

The man looked embarrassed, then chagrined as his friends laughed and made the most of her cool put-down. With thanks and waves, they pushed their friend toward the door.

From behind the book rack, Paul saw Christy look in his direction. "Can I help you with something?" she called, coming around the counter.

He felt the same sense of panic he'd experienced the night before they were supposed to be married. That same sense of feeling like a stranger with a woman with whom he'd thought himself in love.

Only this time *she* was the stranger. This chic, seductive woman wasn't Christine Bowman. This was some...some mutation of Christy who wouldn't have thought about him twice in the twelve years he'd been gone.

As she came closer, something seemed to drop out of his life, something that had lived with him all that time—something he finally considered himself well rid of. Guilt.

This woman hadn't needed him. She'd done fine without him. He didn't have to give her another thought. And he didn't have to apologize.

She was within steps of him when the front door burst open and a young woman rushed in, brown bags toppling out of her arms, soft-drink cups stacked in a precarious column.

"Help!" she shrieked, laughing. "Here's your—Oops!"

Paul had no idea what had fallen to the floor. He knew only that Christy had turned to hurry to the young woman's aid, and he had an opportunity to escape.

He experienced an ironic sense of déjà vu as he hurried down the street in the direction of the old Bertrand family home he would share with his father for the next month or so. Except that he wasn't running away from her this time, he told himself. He was simply avoiding her. Caring for Louis would keep him fairly housebound, and if he was lucky, he would not have to encounter Christy before he left.

It would be better that way. Much better.

INSIDE THE SHOP, Christy and Anita Churchill laboriously picked up pieces of grated cheese and black olives off Honeymoon Hideaway's pink carpeting.

"That's the last time I ask you to bring me a taco salad," Christy said, putting a handful of olives in a paper bag, then holding it open for Anita to do the same. "I'll ask for something that sticks together better, like a peanut-butter sandwich."

Anita sat back on her heels apologetically. "I shouldn't have put the sausage dog between the pastrami on rye and your salad. But I was in a hurry. The deli's swamped. Mom and Dad are screaming orders at each other. They can never decide who's in charge when the rush hits."

Chris pushed her gently, laughing. "Well, go on back. I'll clean this up."

"I'll bring you a fresh salad as soon as the rush is over. But...Chris?"

Chris looked up at her friend's concerned tone.

"Wasn't that...Paul Bertrand?"

Chris felt herself go pale. Her heart gave an erratic jolt. She stared at the open doorway a moment, mouth agape, then pulled herself together and turned to Anita, pretending not to be shocked at the suggestion.

"Where?" she asked calmly.

"In the shop. Walking out as I dropped your salad on the floor."

She'd known there'd been somebody back there behind the books. But when she'd helped Anita pick up the dropped food, he'd apparently left.

She reached under a rack to retrieve a piece of cheese she'd missed. "I don't think so," she replied. "I think I'd have noticed. What would he be doing here, anyway?"

"I heard he's come to take care of Louis. And to be in Mike Barstow's wedding."

Chris got to her feet and made a production of brushing off her dress. "Paul and Louis have been at odds most of Paul's life. I doubt he'd come home to take care of him."

"He is," Anita insisted. "His cousin, Jacqui Powell, told me. In fact, I think she said he was due today." She was silent for one significant moment, then she asked gravely, "What'll you do?"

Chris shrugged a shoulder as she opened the cash register to pay Anita for her lunch—what was left of it. "Nothing," she replied lightly. "So he left me at the altar. That was twelve years ago. It's all water under the bridge."

Anita pushed the money back at Chris and shook her head, giving her a knowing smile. "You don't expect me to believe that for one minute, There's no such thing as water under the bridge to you. You've built a dam over the years to hold back your emotions. And I think you're in for one hell of a flood."

Chris rolled her eyes. "Save the drama for your summer theater group, Nita. I have no feelings for Paul, and he obviously has none for me. After all this time, we probably wouldn't even recognize each other." She tried to force the money on her again. "Take this. The cheese and olives slid off with the lid, but the rest of the salad's intact."

Anita picked up the other two orders and backed away. "On the house today. We still on for dinner Friday night? Hale's got a Kiwanis meeting."

"Sure. Chinese? Italian?"

"Why don't we just go to the Haven Inn? I feel like sitting by the fire and getting stuffed on clam boil and cheesebread."

"Yum. Meet you there at seven."

Chris followed Anita to the door and waved as she disappeared into the print shop with the other two deliveries. She glanced idly up and down First Street, looking for any sign that her friend had been right about Paul Bertrand.

The only man visible was a white-haired old fellow coming out of the nearby law office. If Paul had been in the shop, he was long gone.

Paul. The young man to whom she'd opened her heart, with whom she'd shared kisses. The young man who'd freed the young woman budding beneath the unfashionable intelligence and awkward social skills. He'd handled her trust with knightly tenderness and protection, and she'd fallen desperately in love. Then he'd ripped her heart in two.

She remembered running to the bridge in her wedding dress when it'd become obvious he wasn't coming, and throwing her bridal bouquet into the Sussex River in a poetic gesture of despair.

By the next morning she'd shored up her emotions, gone back to work in her father's department store and presented a brave face to the world.

But under the heroism grew a deadly determination only the minuteman in Soldier's Green would understand. She'd bared her soul and had it kicked. She wanted only one thing out of life, and she didn't care how long it took. Revenge.

If Paul Bertrand was in town, he'd damn well better watch his back.

Chapter One

"Paul!" Louis Bertrand shouted into the contraption he held in his hand, then slapped it when there was no response.

"Yeah?" came an instant later.

"Don't forget the Dijon on my sandwich!"

Downstairs in the kitchen, Paul closed his eyes and dredged up patience. He knew he had to have some somewhere. He'd been his father's nurse for only three days now, and he was already balanced on the brink of insanity.

"Dad, you don't have to shout into the transmitter. I can hear you. And don't hit it. You're going to break the radio. Dijon's already on the tray. What do you want to drink?"

"Moët & Chandon. And please pick a good year."

"You're getting iced tea. Lime?"

On the other end of the two-way radio Paul heard a dramatic sigh and what sounded like a desperate plea to *le bon Dieu*. His father always lapsed into French when he was excited or displeased.

"You can have one drink tonight at the bachelor dinner. Alcohol's not good for you when you're sedentary."

There was another sigh and more French. "Then put me on wheels, please. Skis, blades, ball bearings. Anything!"

Paul hit the Off button, poured a tall glass of tea and added a wedge of lime. He looked over the turkey-pastrami sandwich, the cup of fresh fruit and the medication his father was supposed to have with his meal.

As a nurse and indentured servant, he decided, he wasn't bad. As long as he didn't think about the world-changing events getting by him, he might last the month. All he had to do was tune out his father when he grew insufferable and he'd have it made. That, unfortunately, was easier thought than done. Louis seemed determined to make amends and Paul was equally determined to maintain the rift.

"I appreciate your coming to help me," Louis said as Paul placed the wicker tray on his lap. He was settled on a daybed Paul had pulled up to the bedroom window so that his father could look down over the river.

"So you've said several times," Paul replied, adjusting the blinds to soften the early-afternoon glare. "I'll tell you again that the trip from Boston isn't that far, and I was due for a vacation, anyway."

Louis wasn't deceived for a moment. Paul resented being here, just as he'd known he would. He wished things were otherwise, of course, but that would be asking too much. He'd long ago accepted that a gap existed between them the width of the Atlantic Ocean. He'd intended to do something about it for years, and the broken leg had finally provided the opportunity.

He'd known progress with Paul would be slow. His son had been deeply hurt. But Louis hadn't been prepared for the studied blankness in the boy's eyes, the look that hardly recognized him as a man, much less his father.

Louis had understood the day Paul arrived that subtlety would never work with him, so he'd embarked on a campaign of bold annoyance, determined to elicit a reaction. So far, Paul seemed impervious to it. But he, Louis, had provided the genes with which the boy sustained his determined nonchalance. He had hope.

"Thank you," Louis said. "Good-looking sandwich. Can you stay a minute?"

Paul shook his head. "Got to switch the laundry. You're sure you're up to the bachelor dinner tonight?"

Louis nodded, wincing dramatically as he tried to adjust his leg in its awkward cast under the tray. Paul moved the tray aside, lifted Louis under the arms until he sat up a little higher, then adjusted the wrapped leg comfortably.

"Thank you. I'm looking forward to the dinner." He accepted the tray again and smiled up at his son. "I won't cramp your style, I promise. I'm still enough of a bachelor to know how to behave at these things."

"I never doubted that for a moment." Paul flung the retort dryly, quietly, as he headed for the door.

Something in the set of Paul's shoulders reminded Louis vividly of his mother. How many times had Laurette turned her back on him in just that way?

"Paul!" he said quickly.

He saw the banked impatience as Paul turned at the door. "Yes?"

Louis drew a breath and said before he lost courage, "I wish you were here out of love, rather than duty."

Paul hesitated only an instant. "I'm here because Jacqui has three children, a new marriage and a business to run, and you need a nurse's complete attention."

"You're here because I asked you to come."

"Yes."

"I asked you for a reason."

Paul didn't like the sound of that. His father was directing this conversation to a place he had no intention of going.

"Because I make *tourtière* the way Mother used to make it. What you feel for me is cupboard love. And I have no intention of talking about my mother while I'm here. Is that clear?"

Louis was not discouraged. He'd expected this reaction; he just didn't have to accept it.

"Is that fair?" he asked.

Paul made a scornful sound. "Was anything you did to her fair? Eat your lunch. I'm going downstairs. Call on the radio when you're finished."

Louis watched him walk away, feeling pain and a curious pride in the difficult man he'd sired. He remembered that Paul had defended his mother in just that way twenty years ago when she'd left.

Well. He sipped iced tea and had to force it past a lump in his throat. He'd taken the first step. Though he hadn't gotten very far, he'd opened a door. He grinned to himself. All a good Frenchman ever needed to succeed in any situation was a foot in the door.

THE NOISE LEVEL in the banquet room of the Haven Inn was deafening. The behavior of forty men in a broad range of ages without the civilizing influence of the women in their lives had taken a primitive turn. They drank too freely, talked too loudly, laughed too much.

Paul observed this with less than sober concentration. He'd had too many straight whiskeys, and everything in his life that caused him concern had slipped behind a rosy curtain in his brain. He was feeling mellow and amused and uncharacteristically philosophical. Normally he dealt more with facts than feelings, but tonight he had slipped into a comfortable place where he was free of those confining limitations. He felt like Indiana Jones on the brink of discovery.

"You still have time to reconsider," Danny Tucker was telling Mike Barstow. He leaned across the long table, blond hair falling across his forehead. He whispered conspiratorially, "You can still escape! You don't have to be like us, led to the old ball and chain without recourse. You can follow Paul. He got away!"

There were loud, vaguely slurred cheers. Paul was slapped on the back by those who could reach him and toasted by those who could not.

"Wait a minute. Wait a minute." A young man Paul didn't know held up both hands for attention. There was a swizzle stick in each of them. He frowned, apparently confused. "I like having a wife."

Danny corrected him slowly, distinctly. "You like having a woman. There's a difference. And Paul..." He lifted his glass to him again, and everyone still able to hold one followed suit. "Paul, bless him, *knew* the difference."

Though in town less than a week, Paul had already heard the rumors about Danny's beautiful but demanding wife, and her insistence that he move his law practice to the Cape. Danny's personal grudge in this issue was only faintly veiled by his jocularity.

But in his rosy state, Paul accepted the resultant applause as his due.

"Still..." the young man insisted, hesitating as he seemed to lose the thought, then smiling as it returned. "Still, if he'd been married in Eternity, he'd have had a happy, um...a happy..." He turned to the man next to him. "What do you call it?"

"Marriage?"

"That's it. Marriage. You know the legend." The young man found Paul with his unfocused gaze. "Anyone married in Eternity lives happily ever after. It's proven. It's documented. It's..." He frowned and turned to the sage beside him once again. "What was I saying?"

"Eternity."

The young man looked puzzled for a moment, then nodded. "Eternity. Repent. It's coming."

His companions laughed, and someone went to the restaurant proper in search of a waitress and a pot of coffee.

"I love women," Paul admitted from the depths of his mellow and magnanimous mood. "I just refuse to be trapped by one."

"Hear, hear!" someone shouted. "You did what many of us were tempted to do and didn't have the guts."

"Now I'm free to live as I please, go where I please, do as I please, without a woman demanding that I be 'sensitive' and 'nurturing,' and 'network' with our friends when I'd rather be watching the Sox." The popular buzzwords were slurred.

The cheer that followed that statement was deafening. Still nursing his first gin and tonic, Louis watched his son from the vantage point of sobriety. He saw the boy's position as a dangerous one. He was too superior, too removed, too sure of himself. He was too young to realize how far life stretched beyond the vigor of youth—and how lonely his isolationist strategy would one day make him. That was not what he wanted for Paul. And it was time to do something about it.

Louis reached to the floor where Paul had placed his crutches and stood them up beside his chair.

Paul turned to take them from him. "Where you going?"

"I left my medicine in the car."

Paul watched his father fumble with the crutches, then took them away from him and pushed him gently back into his chair. "I'll get it for you. Where'd you put it?"

Louis checked one coat pocket, then the other. "I'm not sure. I know I had it in my pocket when we left the house and now I can't find it. I must have dropped the bottle on the seat, or under it."

Paul shook his head and noticed that the room seemed to shake with it. "You need a keeper."

Louis smiled broadly. "That's why I sent for you. Thank you, son. Maybe I'll leave you an inheritance, after all."

Paul rolled his eyes. The room rolled, too. "That would be a generous offer if you had anything. Stay put until I get back."

"Of course."

The moment Paul left the room, Louis drew Danny Tucker to his side.

"I have a plan," he said. "And I need your help to carry it out."

"What kind of pan?" Danny asked.

"Plan," Louis enunciated. "I have a *plan*. A little joke on Paul."

As this outrageous idea had begun to form in his mind earlier in the evening, Louis had been concerned about the willingness of Paul's friend to comply. Danny considered Paul such a hero he'd been afraid he might refuse.

But he hadn't counted on his jealousy that Paul was free and he wasn't. Danny listened eagerly, if a little vaguely, as Louis explained the plan.

CHRIS AND ANITA, in a booth at the far end of the inn's dining room, paused in their conversation as another loud chorus of male laughter drifted out of the banquet room.

Anita leaned her chin on a fist and rolled her eyes. "I shudder to think what's going on in there. Poor Mike Barstow is probably being forced to eat raw meat and memorize passages from *Iron John*."

Chris shook her head tolerantly. "What is it about marriage that makes frightened little boys out of big strong men? It's as though they have to act big and laugh loudly to overcome the terror of replacing their poker night with dinner at the in-laws."

Anita attacked her mud pie with concentration. "Who knows? I don't think we'll ever understand. It never occurs to them that we give up a lot, too. Jacqui was right, incidentally."

"About what?"

Anita put down her fork, swallowed and took a sip of coffee. "About Paul being in town. I saw him this morning when I delivered muffins to the video store. He was picking up movies for Louis."

"Really." Chris knew that. Yesterday's *Courier* had carried a small article about his visit to Eternity and listed his various journalism awards. She also knew that he was a member of the bachelor party making so much noise in the other room. She thought she could even isolate the sound of his laughter.

"Don't you want to know how he looks?"

"No."

Anita leaned forward irrepressibly. "He's even better looking than you remember him."

"I don't remember him," Chris insisted. She did, of course, but her memories of him were entangled with various plots for revenge. Ultimately they'd all been discarded as too ugly, too difficult to execute on her own, too likely to earn her life in Leavenworth.

"He has shoulders that won't quit, legs that go on forever, great hair and a smile that stopped my heart."

Chris frowned at her. "You're married."

Anita shrugged guiltlessly. "I was just looking. Now that you're both older, more...more together... maybe you'll—"

"No," Chris said quickly, decisively.

Anita folded her arms on the table and nodded sympathetically. "You were special together. I know he embarrassed you, but—"

"Embarrassment is a passing thing." Chris picked up the table knife and unconsciously tested the blunt tip with her finger. "The pain he caused me lived with me a long, long time. All I want from Paul Bertrand is a strip off his hide."

Anita blinked. "Chris! Revenge isn't healthy."

Chris drew a delicately lethal swath in the air with the knife. "That's the point. I'd like to render him extremely *un*healthy. I felt dead for months. It's only fair."

Anita appeared shocked. "I've never seen this side of you before."

Chris put the knife down and shrugged, a casual smile suggesting that her statement had been nothing more than a joke. Her eyes, however, were deadly serious. "Paul's never come back before."

"You know, I suppose," Anita said cautiously, "that he's probably in the banquet room at Mike Barstow's party. He's an usher at the wedding. He's been in close touch with many of his old friends over the years."

"Yes," Chris said mildly. "I know."

"If I go to the ladies' room, you promise you won't do anything for which I'll have to get you a lawyer and a bondsman?"

Chris smiled, but didn't promise.

Then as Anita headed for the rest room, Chris noticed Louis Bertrand leaning on crutches near the maître d's podium. He tottered dangerously as he freed one arm to beckon her.

She studied him in confusion, then looked behind her to see if he'd truly beckoned *her*. There was nothing behind her but wall.

She pointed a finger at her chest and mouthed "Me?"

Louis nodded vigorously and beckoned her again. She dabbed at her lips with the napkin, then went to join the older man. He gestured with a crutch to an old church pew that served as a bench in the waiting area.

"Louis," Chris scolded before her old friend could say anything, "what are you doing here? Don't tell me you're at the party?" She indicated the room from which loud laughter erupted once again.

He nodded. "I came with Paul." He smiled wickedly. "You remember Paul."

Chris, sitting primly beside him, touched one of the crutches he'd leaned against the bench between them. "That's not funny, Louis. You and I have managed to remain friends, but I could cheerfully pound your son into the ground with one of these. Or maybe both of them."

Louis pinched her cheek. "That's my girl. I love a woman with fire in her soul. I have a plan that will allow you your revenge."

She looked surprised. "Oh? What makes you think I'm interested in revenge?"

Louis waved a hand and smiled. "I think my plan, with your cooperation and the support of a collaborator, will see that my son gets everything that's coming to him."

Chris narrowed her eyes. "That would be too good to be true."

Louis grinned. "Let me explain."

WHEN PAUL WALKED slowly and carefully back into the restaurant, he was surprised to find his father seated on a bench near the maître d's podium.

"I thought I asked you to stay put," he said, frowning. His search for the pills had been futile, and since much of it had been conducted from a nearly upside-down position, he felt even less connected to his surroundings than he had when he'd left. The rosy glow was now bright fuchsia.

His father held up a small brown bottle and smiled apologetically. "Found it in my pants pocket. Sorry. But look who's here!"

Paul focused on the beautiful brunette seated beside his father and wondered where he had seen her before. She was vaguely familiar, but he couldn't remember why. His brain simply wouldn't put it together. But it didn't matter. She was beautiful. And she was smiling at him.

Chris stood and thought that Anita had been right. As an eighteen-year-old boy, Paul Bertrand hadn't been quite this tall. In those days, her gaze had been even with his mouth. Now she looked into the loosened knot of his tie. He hadn't had those shoulders then, either. He'd been well-proportioned, but slender. Time and some kind of exercise had filled him out wonderfully.

Thick brown hair sprang neatly back from a side part over a high forehead. He had dark eyebrows and his nose was straight and strong, his chin square and firm. His dark brown eyes were bloodshot and a little unfocused, but moving over her with determined concentration.

His smile was . . . the same. She felt it like a knife to her midsection. It cut through the protective layers she wore to the heart of the girl who'd once loved him with a seventeen-year-old's fervor.

For a moment she was disoriented. Then Louis cleared his throat, winked at her when she caught his eye, and she remembered what she had to do.

She wrapped both her arms around one of Paul's and leaned close enough to him that their lips were less than a quarter of an inch apart. "Would you like to dance?" she whispered.

He closed the fraction of an inch and kissed her. Chris expected to be revolted. He smelled of whiskey and some expensive cologne and he'd once broken her heart and stomped on the pieces.

She wasn't revolted at all. This authoritative approach to kissing was something else he hadn't had twelve years ago. He'd been gentle and tender, but now he was sure and confident. Even intoxicated, he touched her as though he knew precisely what he was doing and precisely what he wanted. As much as she wanted to hurt him, something within her responded to his certainty.

He drew away and looked into her eyes, a frown line between his brows. "Would you like to come home with me?"

She held his gaze, unwilling to glance at Louis, unwilling to let him suspect.

"Dance first," she said, turning Paul adroitly toward the lounge and the small dance floor there.

They almost collided with Anita, who suddenly appeared from around the corner and stopped in her tracks. She looked from Chris to Paul, then back to Chris again.

"Hi. Are you...is he...What?"

Chris smiled at her. "Would you get my purse and leave it with the maître d', please? I'm staying a little longer."

"But you—"

"I know. But you know what they say about the best-laid plans."

Anita turned to Louis as Chris and Paul disappeared into the lounge, gazing into each other's eyes.

"What happened?" she asked, sitting down beside him. "I mean, you know how she feels about him. A moment ago, when we were talking, she was plotting revenge. What did he do to suddenly change her mind?''

Louis smiled after the pair, a speculative gleam in his eye that changed to concern the longer he stared. He hadn't been entirely honest with Chris. But then, he'd rarely been entirely honest with anyone. It was the role fate had thrust upon him.

Still, the plan had been carefully thought out and developed to benefit everyone involved. Fate could intervene, either as friend or foe. One could never be sure.

He would have to wait and see. He turned to smile at Anita. ''I imagine she's had second thoughts.''

Chapter Two

Chris sat in the upholstered rocker by the window and watched the dawn. The old Bertrand home stood on a small knoll at the far end of First Street where it had once been surrounded by a low stone wall and a birch forest.

The wall in the back remained, hemming in a wild garden, but the front one now sat on the other side of the street that had been paved early in the century. The side walls had become the property of other home-owners when the land was subdivided after the First World War.

Chris had always thought it a wonderful house, even in its current state of dignified disrepair. From this downstairs window she could see broad green lawns and trees just beginning to turn rusty, leaves shimmering in the early-morning breeze.

Louis had rented the house out for years as he'd pursued his theatrical career. Then he'd moved in with Jacqui when he'd come back to Eternity, rather than displace the Pembrook college professor who'd been the current tenant. But the professor had moved away at the end of the summer, and when Paul had arrived to take over Louis's care, they'd moved back into the old Bertrand home.

Chris snuggled into the blanket she'd wrapped around herself and felt her courage fly as the man in the bed turned over. He lay still again, and she watched his profile, handsome even in sleep, and felt an unreasoning anger that he could be so at peace.

After what he'd done to her, his sleep should be haunted even twelve years after the deed.

Courage returned. She could do this. She should do this. She *would* do this.

Paul made a restless sound and moved closer to the side of the bed she'd occupied in the early hours of the morning. His hand, palm open, slid across her pillow.

Resolutely, she dropped the blanket at the foot of the bed and went to slip in beside him as he turned onto his back and dropped an arm over his eyes.

The sheets were cool and his body heat beckoned her. She curled up against him, snuggled into his shoulder and closed her eyes.

PAUL WAS SURE he was dead. He had to be. It was impossible to feel this way and still be among the living. His head vibrated like the aftermath of a crash of cymbals, and his throat felt like a moonscape. Everything hurt, from his toenails to his eyelashes.

He had to get his father's breakfast. He should open his eyes to look at the clock, but he knew that would be a painful experience and he wasn't sure he was up to it.

He stroked her hair and considered his options. He could lie here until his father called for him. The receiver was right here somewhere. He could pretend he hadn't come home last night and let his father order out. He could call Jacqui and tell her that he was sending Louis back to her and that her prolonged honeymoon was over.

He ran his fingers through the long silken strands and let them fall onto his chest, then combed through them again, the action soothing him, relaxing the hellish throbbing behind his eyes.

Then something very subtle in the morning's tableau halted his movements. He closed the hand through which he'd been sifting a woman's hair and tried to engage his brain, despite the banging in his head.

A woman's hair.

Ellie, who sometimes spent the night with him, had hair that fell in a bell shape to just below her ears. When he ran his fingers through it, the pleasure was short-lived. It slipped from his hand, too short to toy with, to grab in a fist.

And Ellie was in Boston.

But there was a length of silk wrapped around his hand. Or he was still caught in the remnant of a dream. Cautiously, he opened his hand and swept his fingers back. A woman's glossy, dark brown hair drifted through his fingers for several seconds before falling away.

Then he became aware of warm softness curled against his side, a light weight across his bare waist and hooked over his thigh.

He opened his eyes to bars of blindingly bright sunlight on the opposite wall. He let his eyes drift down and saw the softly rounded point of a woman's shoulder attached to a graceful arm hooked across his waist. Over all of it was a dark brown tangle of hair catching highlights from the invading sun.

He closed his eyes again and swore to himself. He never brought women home, except Ellie, and that was only because she understood the rules. And he'd certainly had no intention of getting involved with anyone for the short time he'd be in Eternity.

He tried desperately to remember last night. But all his clouded memory would show him was toast after toast of straight whiskey to his expertise at avoiding women and marriage. If those men around the table could only see him now. He'd be dethroned in an instant.

He couldn't remember that there'd been a woman involved last night. In fact, during the early part of the evening which he could remember, he and . . . the men at Mike's party—that was it! Mike's party!—had been cheering their purely masculine company.

A vague recollection tried to surface of his father on a bench with a woman beside him, but as he reached for it, it drifted away. No matter, he thought, resigned. He'd have to wake her up, explain briefly and clearly that the night was over and send her on her way.

As he opened his eyes to do just that, he felt the weight against his side shift slightly to his chest. She was awake. She'd crossed her arms on his chest and was looking into his face. That tangled skein of hair obscured her features, except for the tip of a delicate nose.

"Hi," a sleepy, husky voice said.

Then she swept a hand over her face, moving the hair aside, and his heart gave a startled lurch. He was staring into lazy blue eyes focused on him in adoration.

Christy!

She braced her hands on either side of him on the mattress and pushed herself up his body until they were eye to eye, their lips inches apart. "Paul," she whispered, her gaze going over him as though he'd hung the moon.

Something about this—about being this close to her—jangled a memory from the night before that receded when he pursued it.

He let it go. This morning she didn't look like the sophisticated woman he'd seen in the Honeymoon Hideaway yesterday afternoon. Without makeup and with that look of love in her eyes, she was the old Christy who'd adored him, who'd hung on his every word.

For a minute he was the old Paul—flattered by her trust, buoyed by her confidence. The last twelve years were swept away and he was eighteen again and desperate to make love to her.

He caught a fistful of her hair, pulled her down to his pillow and opened his mouth over hers. He kissed her with all the uncontrolled passion of a teenage boy, all fire and feeling and little skill.

Then he felt her arms twine around his neck and her leg hitch up against him, and the man in him took over, sensitive to that little surrender, eager to consider her pleasure, as well as his own.

Chris's heart beat like the wings of a hummingbird. He'd rolled over, and she was trapped under him as she'd always dreamed of being, first as a girl longing to make love with the man who would become her husband, then as a woman, planning insidious revenge. She would lure him to her bed, then cast him aside when it would hurt him the most.

But she didn't seem to have a plan at the moment. His hands, his lips, wouldn't allow coherent thought to form. He was so much better at this than she remembered, slower and more tender.

She reached a hand up to touch his face—and he stopped abruptly, catching her wrist in his hand and pulling her up with him to a sitting position.

He held her hand up in front of her face and put his index finger to the gold band on her ring finger. "You're married!" he accused, anger clearing his brain.

She smiled brightly, and reached her right hand to hook it around his neck and draw him closer. "Yes. Isn't it wonderful?"

"Christy!" He pushed her away, his brow darkening, his dawning awareness trying to sort through details he couldn't seem to bring together. "What in the hell are you doing here?"

She blinked, her smile slipping just a little. "You brought me here. Don't you remember?"

He tried—and failed. "No, I don't remember."

She grinned wickedly. That was an expression she'd never had in the old days. "How can you have been so magnificent and not remember?"

He put his free hand to the pain in his forehead. It wasn't like him not to remember a sexual encounter.

"I was drunk," he said.

She leaned forward to kiss his cheek. "You were divine."

Chris was beginning to enjoy herself. The expression on Paul's face was priceless. His hair was ruffled, his jaw bearded, his eyes bleak with the pain of what must be a hangover of monstrous proportions. Unfortunately the "morning after" had done nothing to diminish his wonderful shoulders and beautifully defined pectorals.

This moment was everything she'd dreamed of. And she'd be able to savor it for some time.

She pulled her hand from his slack grasp and wound her arms around him, sending them both back to the pillows.

"Come on, darling," she said, nipping at his earlobe. "One more time, then I'll make breakfast."

He pushed her away and got to his feet, pulling on a pair of jeans, then pausing with a hand braced on the dresser, holding his head with the other.

She pulled the blankets up to her chin, amazed at her theatrical potential as she feigned a hurt expression and asked in an injured tone, "Paul, darling, what is it?"

He turned to her and leaned against the dresser wearily.

"Christy." He winced, as though even talking hurt. "I don't know what happened. I don't remember. But you're married and I don't play around with married women."

"Paul, you didn't play around," she teased. "You were very serious."

"Christy..."

"Oh, Paul, it's all right." She knelt on the mattress and reached out to catch his left hand. She held it up to him as he'd done to her. A gold band that matched the one on her third finger winked in the sunlight. He'd bought her ring twelve years ago, the same day she'd bought his. But he didn't remember. "I'm married to *you*."

It took him a full minute to absorb and understand what she'd told him. Then he straightened away from the dresser and said flatly, "What?"

"We got married, remember? In the Eternity Chapel. Your father and Anita Churchill stood up for us."

Terror struck at the very heart of Paul's body and soul. Married? Bound? Incarcerated? Emasculated? No!

Then he said it aloud. "No. I did not get married last night. If I'd gotten married, I'm sure I'd know."

Chris wrapped the sheet around her and struggled off the bed, following him as he marched into the kitchen.

"Paul, think!" she said urgently. "We met again in the restaurant. I was sitting on the bench with your father and you'd just come in from outside. You'd been searching the car for his pills or something."

Paul opened the freezer to extract a bag of coffee beans and stood in the open door a moment, letting the frigid air hit his face. He did have a vague memory of his father and a bench—and a woman.

"We danced," she went on, following him as he moved to the counter and poured beans into the coffee grinder. "Then you took me out to look at the moon."

She took him by the arms and turned him toward her, her eyes wide and dreamy. "We danced outside, then you held me and told me how much you've missed me, how much you regret leaving me."

"No." He pulled easily out of her grasp, then enclosed her in his own. Then he shook her for good measure. "I do *not* regret leaving here. I do not regret *not* getting married!"

She blinked at him. "Then why did you marry me last night?"

"I didn't!" he shouted, then immediately regretted that as his head vibrated with the sound.

"Then why are you wearing a ring?" she asked reasonably.

He looked down at her, swaddled in the paisley sheet like some Arab slave girl, and entertained a new suspicion. All earlier thoughts of apologizing to her fled.

"You put it there," he accused.

She admitted it without hesitation. "It's customary during a wedding ceremony."

He turned away from her in disgust, the sudden movement also jarring his head. He held it together with both hands.

"Why don't you go take a shower," she suggested gently, "and I'll make the coffee. Something tells me you'd never survive grinding the beans."

He considered that a wonderful idea. He stopped at the door to the kitchen to turn and say with conviction, "I did *not* get married last night."

She blew him a kiss as she fussed with a box of filters. "Check the bathroom mirror," she said, then shooed him on his way.

Chris watched him walk away, smiling over how well it was going, then frowning at the realization of how forcefully he did *not* want to be married to her.

It was very unflattering, but in this particular case, it was only fuel for the plan. She hummed as the coffee grinder filled the small kitchen with noise and aroma.

" 'THIS IS TO CERTIFY that Paul Louis Bertrand and
Christine Camille Bowman were joined in Holy Matrimony on the fifteenth day of September, Nineteen
Hundred and . . .' Oh, God.'' Paul studied the parch-
ment that had been tucked into the frame of the bathroom mirror and saw the horrifyingly legal notary seal
right beside the Eternity Chapel sunburst seal.

He was married! To Christy, whom he'd barely escaped with his will intact once before. He hadn't been
as lucky this time.

This was his father's fault, he thought as he tossed
the certificate onto the counter and tore the shower
curtain back. If his father hadn't called and asked him
so pathetically to come home and take care of him,
Mike Barstow would never have asked him to usher at
his wedding, and he wouldn't have become intoxicated at the Haven Inn, ripe for what he was now
convinced was Christy Bowman's plot for retribution.

There had to be a way out. He was sure it would
come to him when he'd had his shower and gotten
dressed.

The shower was beating on the tight muscles between his shoulder blades when it came to him. An-
nulment. And if that was impossible, divorce. So he'd
have the shortest marriage on record. That was fine
with him.

He turned the shower off, pushed the curtain aside,
and found Christy holding a towel open for him. She'd
abandoned the sheet for green corduroy pants and a
green-and-pink sweater. Her hair was tied off to the
side in a ponytail adorned with some ruffly thing the
same color as her pants.

Her eyes were soft and smiling as he yanked the towel from her and wrapped it around himself. She picked up the certificate and traced a hand lovingly over their names.

"You put it on the bathroom mirror," she said softly, "because you said it was the first thing you wanted to see in the morning—after me."

Something occurred to him and he stabbed the air triumphantly with his index finger.

"The license! It takes five days to get one in the Commonwealth of Massachusetts."

She shrugged apologetically. "Not when one's godfather is a judge."

He studied her suspiciously, then had to believe she was telling the truth. Her family and their friends would charm the law for one another. He groaned, hands on the towel that covered his hips. "How can I be absolutely sure you're not snowing me?"

"Snowing you?"

"Yeah. Exacting revenge."

Her eyes grew wider and more innocent. "Revenge for what?"

He folded his arms and found himself having to look away from those eyes. They were as sweet and innocent—and hurt—as he'd remembered them all these years. He focused on the little pleat between her eyebrows. "For leaving you at the altar."

She laughed softly and waved a casual hand. "That was so long ago." Then she took a step forward and wrapped her arms around his waist. "And last night made up for everything, anyway."

"Christy..." He took her arms and put her firmly away from him. "You have to understand. I can't do this."

"Paul," she said gently, "it's done. We're wearing each other's rings—the rings we bought together twelve years ago. The license is recorded, the certificate is right there."

"I was drunk," he insisted. "I'm sure it doesn't count."

She shook her head. "You seemed very coherent at the time. You repeated the vows, you signed your name, you even signed the bet."

"We're having it annulled."

"We can't. I mean, we've . . ."

"Then we're getting a divorce."

She expelled a heartfelt sigh, then turned away, apparently finally resigned. "All right. If you're sure that's what you want."

"That's what I want."

She stopped at the door to say desultorily, "Come and eat when you're ready. Breakfast is warming in the oven. I've already fed your father and he's watching a movie."

"Thank you."

It wasn't until the door closed behind her that his mind registered what she'd said. He'd "signed the bet"?

"WHAT BET?" he asked as he walked into the kitchen.

Chris glanced up from pouring coffee into his cup and refused to let herself react to the gorgeous sight of him in jeans and a plain white sweater. His dark good looks stood out dramatically, the suspicious anger in his eyes darkening them further.

She pulled out the chair and gestured for him to sit down. "The bet you made with your father and the other men at the bachelor party. Something about your car.''

"My car?" Concern battled with the sight of her shapely bottom as she leaned into the oven to remove his breakfast. She placed sausage and eggs before him and pulled off the oven mitt.

"Yes," she replied, narrowing her eyes as she concentrated on recalling the details. "When you took me into the banquet room to announce that we were about to be married, the men bet you wouldn't stay married, even if we got married at the Eternity Chapel. You bet them your car that you would."

The sight and aroma of sausage and eggs done to perfection, and toasted Portuguese sweet bread, was suddenly sickening. He wanted to doubt her, but he'd doubted her over the wedding, then discovered the wedding certificate.

"I bet my Viper?" he asked in disbelief.

She nodded, rubbing his shoulder consolingly. "But I think you put a time limit on it. A month, I believe. Something like that. Your father's holding all bets and a copy of the rules signed by everyone. You should check with him."

He noticed something slightly out of tune here as she walked away. He caught her wrist and she turned to raise an inquiring eyebrow at him.

"If you did marry me for love," he said quietly, "and I did make this bet, I should think you'd be offended, yet you're taking it awfully well."

She smiled. "That's because I know all I need is a month." She lifted his face and leaned down to kiss him slowly. Then she straightened and winked. "Then you'll be so in love with me you'll change your mind about escaping marriage. We'll be renewing our wedding vows on our fiftieth anniversary in the Eternity Chapel." She squeezed his hand before she pulled away. "Gotta go. The movers just pulled into the driveway."

Paul went back to his breakfast, then looked up with a start. Movers?

"I WAS NOT DRUNK," Louis denied vehemently, aiming the remote control at the television and silencing the old Humphrey Bogart film. "You limited me to one drink, remember? *You* were the one who was foxed."

"Then why didn't you stop me?" Paul fell into the chair at a right angle to the daybed on which his father lay, crutches on the floor beside him.

"You assured me last night that you wanted to get married!"

"You know me better than that."

There was an instant's silence, then Louis said quietly, "I don't know you at all. That's why I asked you to spend time with me."

Paul eased his throbbing head back against the chair cushion and asked reasonably, "Then if you wanted me to spend time with you, why did you let me get married?"

"Because you assured me we'd keep the same arrangement. Me upstairs. You and Chris downstairs. Until the babies start coming, of course, then we'll have to—"

Paul shot Louis a lethal glance. "Don't even say the word 'babies.' There will be no babies. There will be no marriage."

"I'm afraid that's a fait accompli."

"Yeah, well, it may be a done deed in actuality, but the spirit of the thing will remain undone."

Louis studied him in concern. "You mean, you haven't, ah...?" A wave of his hand finished the question.

Paul closed his eyes and groaned. "We have. That is, she says we have. I don't remember, myself. And she's wearing that glow women wear when you've...made them happy."

Louis nodded and smiled distractedly as though he knew the look very well.

Paul groaned, reaching toward his father for the paper that rested on the arm of the sofa. "Let me see that again."

Louis handed him the details of the bet. It had been written on the back of a Haven Inn menu—apparently in his own intoxicated hand.

I, Paul Bertrand, promise to remain married to Christine Bowman for a month's time or forfeit ownership of my Dodge Viper. In the event that I break this promise, my doubting friends will draw for title of the car. If I win, I claim the four thousand dollars contributed by the opposing parties in this negotiation.

Paul Bertrand

Mike Barstow, Witness.

Louis Bertrand, Witness.

This document, too, was notarized.

"You know," Louis said conversationally, "considering what you put her through when you left her at the altar, I'm surprised she'd have you.''

Paul frowned, his gaze unfocused. ''I suspected in the beginning that it was just a plot to get back at me. But there's a notarized wedding certificate from the Eternity Chapel downstairs, and—'' he waved the bet in the air, then leaned forward to put it back on the arm of the sofa ''—there's this.''

There was a loud thump from downstairs and a shouted curse, followed by loud laughter.

''What's happening down there?'' Louis asked.

Paul pushed himself to his feet and stretched his back muscles. ''She's moving in,'' he said grimly. ''I seem to be well and truly trapped. At least for a month.''

Louis smiled up at him. ''Maybe you'll find you like it. Maybe you'll decide to move back to Eternity and buy the *Courier* as the two of you planned to do originally.''

''Not a chance.'' He checked the coffee carafe Christy had left on the small table near the daybed and, finding it empty, picked it up with the rest of the breakfast dishes. ''I promised you one month, and apparently I promised my greedy friends the same. On October fourteenth, I'm out of here.''

''Just like that?''

''Just like that. I'll be back with more coffee.''

Louis smiled as Paul disappeared down the stairs. For a son who purported not to care about his father, he was an attentive nurse. And for a man who claimed not to care for a woman, his eyes were turbulent when he spoke of her.

There was no way of determining how this would all turn out. Paul was a stubborn man. Got that from his mother. But it was clear this would be a very interesting month.

Chapter Three

She was that other Christy now. The two personas seemed to be as clearly delineated as night and day. The fresh-scrubbed young woman with the earnest eyes had been replaced by a woman dressed and groomed as though a photographer for *Vogue* magazine awaited.

Her makeup appeared lightly applied, but it gave a more formal and glamorous appearance to the elegant contours of her face. A misty color on her eyelids brought out the bright blue of eyes framed by thick dark lashes. Her mouth was a darker pink than the long-sleeved wool dress with the flared skirt.

Her hair had been knotted at the nape of her neck, and she sported a pink, shallow-crowned, small-brimmed hat that matched the dress and her high-heeled shoes.

She smiled at him as he helped her out of the Viper. "Aren't weddings wonderful?" she asked, pointing to the groups of people hurrying toward the chapel. "And isn't it great to be part of a community that specializes in making it a lifetime joy for the bride and groom?"

"You enjoy a share in the profits," he observed practically. "No wonder you're enthused."

She shook her head at his dampening reply. "I was speaking as a woman, not a shopkeeper."

"Right," he said, clearly doubtful. He walked her up the steps, then put her in the capable hands of Mike Barstow's brother, Ben. "I'm on duty on the side aisle. See you at the reception." Before he turned away, because Ben seemed to be waiting for it, he leaned down to plant a quick kiss on her lips.

The wedding was mercifully swift, everyone in attendance in remarkably good form, Paul thought, considering the condition they'd been in the night before. And all their brave talk of male dominance and independence seemed to be for naught this afternoon.

Most of the men who'd cheered his escape from matrimony around the banquet table at the Haven Inn had women on their arms today. Danny Tucker himself had his arm around a beautiful but severe-looking little blonde.

Even his father, who'd been picked up by Jacqui and Brent, was being assisted out of the church by a smiling gray-haired woman whose hat brim was pinned back by a sunflower. They were whispering and laughing together.

He could hardly blame any of them, Paul realized guiltily, spotting the wedding ring on his finger. Their hero had fallen.

IT WAS HARD TO BELIEVE, Paul thought, that the men attending the reception that followed at the Haven Inn were the same group who'd attended the bachelor party. Their behavior was decorous and impeccable.

And the music was loud enough to threaten a return of the worst moments of his hangover. He found a quiet corner behind the table of wedding gifts and sipped coffee.

"Paul Bertrand?"

Paul looked up, his expression politely cool in an attempt to discourage conversation, and found himself being studied by a complete stranger in his late teens. He wore the requisite suit and tie, and wire-rimmed glasses over eyes that shone with intelligence.

Interested, Paul put his cup down, stood and offered his hand. "Yes."

"Alex Powell," the young man said, looking eager and embarrassed at the same time. "I'm a cousin a couple of times removed from 'the ladies.'"

"The ladies" Alex referred to were the four Powell sisters, all single and in their seventies. They were direct descendants of William Powell, who'd built the Powell chapel one hundred and fifty years before. They owned the estate that also housed the chapel and the museum.

"You're my hero," Alex went on, still pumping his hand.

Paul grinned. Apparently word hadn't gotten around to the younger generation that he'd fallen from grace.

"You write the cleanest, sharpest pieces in journalism today," Alex went on. "Our teacher's always comparing you to Hemingway. I want to be just like you."

Paul couldn't help but be flattered. "Thank you. I appreciate that. I'd been working so hard just before I came home there wasn't time to slow down, rewrite or figure out if I was even making sense."

"Mr. Cummings says he'll be surprised if you aren't nominated for a Pulitzer for your series on Bosnian children."

Paul shook his head grimly, remembering what he'd seen. "Well, that was hardly my motive at the time. You planning a career in the newspaper business?"

Alex shrugged. "It doesn't look like I'll have the money for college this year. I've applied for a scholarship, but the competition for those is thick, and my math grades have pulled my average down to a B. I'll probably get a job here after school and work on my novel."

"A job with the *Courier*?"

Alex shook his head. "My girlfriend's parents own a supermarket and deli. Mr. Silva said he'd give me a job."

Paul nodded, seeing a trace of something he recognized in the boy's eyes—a very quiet desperation. "Maybe you'll get lucky and the scholarship will come through."

Alex shrugged again. "Maybe. Heard you married Chris Bowman last night. Does that mean you'll be staying in Eternity?"

Paul eyed him with amused suspicion. "This wouldn't be an interview for the high school paper, would it?"

Alex looked sheepish. "Not subtle enough, was I?"

"Try to sound more conversational. 'I understand you were married last night.' Then let me answer that. Nine times out of ten I'll tell you what you want to know without your having to ask. If I don't, try something like 'Can we ask you to judge our year-end news-story contest?' I presume the school still does that?"

"Yes, it does."

"Then I have to agree to do it and you've lined up someone to judge the contest and you'll be a hero among the faculty, or I have to tell you I'll have left Eternity to go back to Boston by then, and you'll have what you need for your article."

"Right. Awesome." Alex seemed impressed, then he assumed a casual stance and asked coolly, "So, can we ask you to judge our year-end news-story contest?"

Paul laughed. "Sorry, I'll be back in Boston by then. But that was a smooth try."

"You mean, Chris is closing the shop and moving with you to Boston?" Alex asked, obviously startled.

Paul fought annoyance at his general carelessness—both in getting himself involved with a woman and in forgetting today that he had to play the role assigned him or lose his car. And the Viper was more than a car. It symbolized what freedom had done for him. While other men his age were driving around in station wagons, minivans or economy imports, he had freedom of the road in a high-performance, two-passenger muscle car. There was no room in it for Boy Scout troops or the family dog. He ignored the fact that he'd just used it to drive a woman to a wedding.

"I haven't planned that far ahead." Chris's voice, quietly sensuous, preceded her graceful movement to his side. She carried a flat purse in one hand, a glass of champagne in the other. "It was all such a surprise. All I know is I don't want to be separated from him."

The brim of her hat brushed Paul's chin as she gazed into his eyes, hers alight with smoky passion.

"Isn't that just like something out of a movie?" A little brunette in an outrageous outfit that combined a lacy blouse, a patterned vest and a short skirt under which she wore silky white leggings that stopped at her ankles, hooked an arm in Alex's. "They're star-crossed lovers, you know. It's destiny that they be together."

Paul saw a subtle change in Chris's expression. The girl's remarks caused a slightly jaded and coolly ironic shadow to drift across the adoration. Then her eyelashes fell and rose again and the shadow was gone.

"Darling, I'd like you to meet Erica Silva. She's an A student at Eternity High and following in our footsteps on the school paper. She also works for me part-time. Her sister is Anita Churchill. She and Ben Churchill were in our art class, remember? We redesigned the paper's masthead together?"

He remembered. He offered his hand to the young woman, who shook his with confident firmness.

"Anita and Ben talk about you all the time," she said, sparkling with effusion. "I can't believe you got married last night. I mean, Chris spends all her time helping *other* people get married and always said she'd never do it. I mean, she never talks about it, and I'm too young to really remember, but Anita told me it's because you..."

It apparently occurred to Erica that it was probably not good manners to remind him the morning after his wedding that he'd once walked out on his bride the night before their original wedding date without telling her he was leaving.

She stammered and blushed. "B-because you...and she didn't...or maybe..."

Alex shot Paul an apologetic male-to-male look, then said quietly to Erica, "You can be quiet now."

She subsided with a sigh and grinned sheepishly. "I talk too much. Usually without thinking. Ask any-body."

"You don't have to ask anybody." Chris laughed lightly. "I can verify that that's true. But all's well that ends well, I always say." She squeezed Paul's arm and looked up at him. "It doesn't matter what happened the first time. You've obviously had second thoughts and here we are—Mr. and Mrs. Paul Bertrand. And I'm so happy."

Chris could not believe how well this was going or how gifted she was proving to be at drama. Of course, she shouldn't be surprised. She'd convinced her family and the entire town that she'd gotten over Paul with her emotions intact. No one suspected that he'd killed every dream she'd ever had for herself.

Though he smiled gallantly at Erica as she apolo-gized and he assured her she had no reason to, Chris felt the tautening of his upper body muscles. He was trapped—at least temporarily—and hating it. She couldn't remember when she'd had a better time.

Paul looked beyond his companions and noticed a lineup of men at the champagne fountain, watching him and Christy with speculative grins. Most of them had been present at the bachelor party. They whis-pered together and pointed with obvious satisfaction.

Friends were fickle, he thought resentfully. Last night, when there hadn't been a woman in sight, he'd been their hero. Today, because he was caught in the grip of the woman who'd somehow tricked him into going to the altar and encouraged him to bet his car, he was fair game for ridicule.

"Excuse us," he said to the young couple as he took Chris firmly by her elbow and looked at her, his eyes holding a veiled threat. "I believe this is my dance, Mrs. Bertrand."

She smiled intrepidly and batted her eyelashes. "And every one hereafter."

The band played something smooth and romantic as Paul drew her into the area reserved for dancing and pulled her into his arms.

She stopped him long enough to remove the single pin that secured her hat, then, holding it in the hand on his shoulder, rested her cheek against his. The lineup of men considering the odds on their bet looked vaguely troubled as he wrapped both arms around her waist.

Chris was surprised by the action. Kids and passionate newlyweds danced that way. She didn't expect that he would. She drew her head back to look into his eyes. Then as he turned her, she saw his friends and understood what he was up to.

Annoyance flickered inside her, then she joined both her hands on the hat she held behind him and swayed with him to the dreamy music. Playing into his hands, she realized, would only help her own cause. As far as she was concerned, this little comic opera could end one of two ways. She would drive him wild with her clinging and wifely adoration until he forfeited the bet and lost his precious Viper, or he would succumb to her charms, at which point she would tell him precisely what she thought of him—and how she'd deceived him—and he would lose his precious pride. Either way, she won.

His hand at the small of her back, pulling her closer to him, startled her out of her plans for retribution. She became sharply aware of the firm contours of his body and the soft pliancy of hers. He'd locked them

together from breast to knee, and every little cell in her
body in contact with him seemed to have developed a
pulse of its own.

Paul felt her ticking heartbeat against his ribs and
tried to grip the anger he felt in both hands. But his
arms were full of her, and he was finding it difficult to
think of anything else.

He remembered the prom and slow dancing with her
in a corner of the high school gym. She'd melted
against him as she did now, and he'd been close to
complete loss of control. Only her insistence that neither of them was prepared, and her idealistic belief
that their first night together should be spent as husband and wife, had prevented him from making love
to her. Caught in her fervor, he'd asked her to marry
him, instead.

Frustration and irritation rose in him side by side.
He'd have pulled out of her arms, but his friends were
watching. So, instead, he tugged at the knot of hair at
the nape of her neck and tilted her head back. As
much to punish her as to unsettle his friends, he kissed
her with all the passion the crowded dance floor would
allow.

Over her shoulder he saw his friends disperse to re-
join their families, their brows knitted with concern.

She stayed close to him when the crowd of women
gathered for the toss of the bridal bouquet. She
cheered when Erica caught it and waved it in the air,
jumping triumphantly. Then Erica flew into Alex's
arms with it, and everyone applauded them.

Alex, Paul thought, looked a little panicky despite
his smile. The people of Eternity were doing to the boy
what they'd done to him. He and Erica were fresh and
young and obviously a perfect match. It was pre-

sumed that they would be. Whatever personal dreams Alex or Erica had went unnoticed. The small-town ethic of "find a nice girl and settle down" had guided them into its little box and locked them in with its seal of approval.

CHRIS SAT QUIETLY beside Paul on the ride home, her hat in her lap, her head resting against the upholstery. The fragrance of fall drifted through the open window as dusk settled over Eternity.

That disturbing sense of having come home turned idly inside him as he drove down Elm Street. Being in a car with Chris was so familiar, only in those days it had been a blue VW bug. And she had been a plain little thing with a lively intelligence and an ability to write headlines that summed up a story in four simple words. He'd admired and resented that about her.

A curious comfort stole over him as he smelled fragrant wood smoke and the tang of the ocean spreading out to infinity at the other end of town. He fought it. This wasn't home. This "marriage" was not in his future.

"Did you ever take that cruise?" Chris asked lazily.

He frowned at the windshield. "Cruise?"

"Don't you remember?" she asked, turning her head to catch his glance. "Even though we could only afford Martha's Vineyard for a honeymoon, we promised ourselves we'd go to the Bahamas on our fifth anniversary. Then we'd start having children."

He did remember, now that she'd reminded him. They used to talk about it every time they went to the beach. It had been part of The Plan—get married, work for a couple of years and save every dime, buy the newspaper, double the advertising with superior reporting and increased circulation, and on and on. Their dreams had had no limits.

"No," he replied a little wearily, the memory causing a drain on what little good humor he'd managed to scrape together during the afternoon. "There never seems to be enough time for long vacations."

She patted his knee in a gesture that seemed purely platonic. His body didn't seem to know that, however. He forced himself to concentrate on the road.

"Doesn't matter," she said. "You don't have the children yet, either, so I guess there's still time." Then she sat up and asked curiously, "Or do you? We didn't get around to that last night. Have you been married?"

He rolled his window down all the way and let in the cool, fragrant air. He was beginning to feel too big for the car. "No. Marriage takes time."

"Last night," she said quietly, "it took all of twenty minutes."

"I mean," he corrected, "living the marriage takes time. And I'm often off at a moment's notice, gone for weeks and out of touch much of the time. When I'm home, I work until all hours."

"You explained that last night." Chris put her hand back to massage his neck at the base of his hairline. "I told you I'd be happy to wait around for you. I'll get someone to run the shop, and open another one in Boston."

"Christy…" They had to talk about this again. She simply wasn't getting the message.

But before he could launch into a repeat of the "I'm not doing this" speech he'd delivered that morning, she leaned forward against her seat belt and said unhappily, "Uh-oh!"

He stared ahead, trying to see what had prompted that sound of foreboding. Through the gathering darkness, he saw a white late-model Cadillac in his driveway.

"Who is that?" he asked.

She leaned back with a groaning sigh. "My parents."

"WHAT IN THE HELL makes you think you can walk into my daughter's life and pick up where you left off?" Nathaniel Bowman confronted Paul in the middle of the Bertrand living room.

Nate owned a department store, though to Paul he'd always looked as though he should quarterback for Notre Dame. That formidable body in an unstructured designer suit lent him an air of sophistication, but inside was a temper under full sail. Paul had always had a lot of respect for the man in the old days, and in deference to that and because he didn't blame him one bit, he stood quietly and let him rail.

"Do you have any idea what you did to her?" Nate demanded. "Can you imagine the humiliation she suffered? The personal trauma? The pain?"

"Daddy..." Chris tried to pull on his arm.

Nate shook her off. "I'm talking."

"You're yelling," she corrected.

"She cried for twenty-four hours!" her father roared. "While her mother and I stood by helpless to say or do anything—"

"Nattie..." Jerina Bowman pulled her daughter aside and stepped between Paul and her husband.

Nate stepped around her. Paul felt required to follow.

"We couldn't make her understand that, just because a creep had walked out on her, her life wasn't over!"

Paul drew a shallow breath, shifted his weight and listened. In a curious way, there was something therapeutic about the experience. He knew he'd had this coming for a long, long time.

"Do you know what she did?" Nate demanded, reaching an arm out for Chris. She walked into it, muttering softly, "Daddy, will you please—?"

Ignoring her, Nate told him. "She came to work for me for a year, just as bright and cheerful as you please, then she enrolled at SMU, got her degree in business and opened her own place. She's important in this town, and she accomplished that not only without you, but in spite of what you did to her."

As Nate paused for breath, Chris said quickly, "Daddy, we're married now."

Nate rounded on her. "I know that! That's why we're here! We leave town for a few days and what happens? Our one and only child marries a rotter while we're away! What is *wrong* with you? Have you no sense? Didn't you stop to think what—"

Paul took Nate's trunklike arm in a firm grip and turned him around. The man bristled like an angry lion.

"I believe your fight's with me and not with her," Paul said. "This is our house, and my father is ill upstairs. I'd appreciate it if you'd keep your voice down."

"Don't you tell me—"

Chris came from behind her father to place herself again between him and Paul. She *was* enjoying Paul's discomfort, though he was bearing up with impressive dignity. But she didn't want things to come to blows.

"That's enough!" Jerina looped both arms in her husband's and pulled him toward the sofa, then pushed him onto it. She straightened the short jacket of her casual denim suit and said politely, "A cup of coffee would be nice about now, Paul."

"I'll get it," Chris offered.

Jerina caught her arm. "No. I'd like to talk to you." She smiled coolly at Paul, and there was more threat in the gesture than amiability. "I'm not as loud as Nattie, but I'm twice as mean. I'd like a few words with her alone."

Surprised and a little confused by Paul's defense of her a moment ago, Chris gave him a nod of reassurance. "Go ahead. I'll explain everything."

Good, he thought as he pushed his way into the kitchen. Because he didn't remember enough to explain.

Chris's mother pushed her onto the sofa beside her father, then sat on the edge of the coffee table, facing her. She took her hands in hers and held them firmly.

"I just want to know one thing," she said.

"I want to know a lot of things!" Nate growled. "I want to—"

Jerina silenced him with a look. She turned her attention back to her daughter. "It isn't like you to make such life-and-death decisions impulsively," she said gently. "I want to know that you weren't coerced in any way. That he didn't bully you into this, or somehow..."

Chris shook her head before her mother had even stopped. Explaining to her parents was a detail she hadn't anticipated when she'd leapt so eagerly on Louis's plan. She'd known her parents were out of town for several weeks, and she'd felt fairly certain the marriage would be over, one way or the other, before they returned. Explaining her victory after the fact would have been a joke they'd have all enjoyed.

Telling them the truth now, when they were so obviously upset and Paul just feet away, simply wasn't feasible. So she did the only thing she could.

"He hasn't threatened or coerced me into marriage," she said honestly. "He came home to take care of Louis because he fell and broke his leg."

Nate snickered. "I heard it was because he leapt from Laura Pratt's second-story bedroom window when her husband came home."

Chris drew a breath for patience. "He turned his foot on the Town Hall steps and fell. I have that on good authority from Anita Churchill, because Ben was the paramedic on duty that day."

"Go on," Jerina encouraged with a glare at her husband.

"Well…" Chris lowered her eyes as she thought. It was hard to lie to her mother. In the old days, it had been virtually impossible. The woman read her like a book. But when Chris looked up, her false facts in order, she saw in her mother's eyes that she was willing to believe anything. She'd loved Paul like a mother twelve years ago, and she'd been thrilled at the prospect of having him for a son-in-law.

"He came home," Chris said, delving into some deep-down stratum of consciousness that held long-suppressed fantasies, "and he was at Mike Barstow's bachelor party last night at the Haven Inn. I was having dinner there with Anita."

Jerina nodded, leaning unconsciously toward Chris.

"I ran into him while I was chatting with Louis, who was also at the party. He asked me to dance..." She shrugged, lost in her own fanciful spell. "Then he kissed me, and told me that he's always loved me, that he's never forgotten me, but he was too ashamed of what he'd done to me to get in touch. Then Louis called and asked him to come home, and he knew what he had to do. He was drawn to me, he said. He thought it was destiny—just a little late. Then he asked me to marry him."

Tears had pooled in her mother's eyes. That made Chris straighten out of her reverie. "He had a license, we found Bronwyn and..." She indicated their faded Victorian surroundings. "And here we are."

Jerina sniffed, then asked pointedly, "But are you happy? Do you really want this, or is it just that you can't stand things that don't work out your way—even twelve-year-old issues?"

"I think it's idiotic and self-destructive," Nate said.

Jerina turned to say gently, "But it's not your life, it's hers. You can't make this turn out the way you think it should, no matter how much you'd like to."

"This was my decision." Chris squeezed her mother's hands and leaned forward to hug her. "This is what I've always wanted." Chris smiled boldly, ignoring the fact that each of them attached a different significance to those words.

Paul came out with a tray bearing a rose-pattered china coffeepot and four cups and saucers. Jerina stood so that he could place it on the coffee table, then she pushed him gently aside.

"I'll be Mother and pour," she said, "since I guess I am now, anyway. Welcome to the family, Paul."

"Mrs. Bowman, I..." Paul began. Chris didn't like the tone of his voice. It had an explanatory quality, as though he intended to divulge that he didn't remember marrying her daughter and that he was staying with her for one month only because of a bet.

Chris reached an arm toward him, desperate to save her plan. "Come sit by me, darling."

Paul resisted her invitation, taking a steaming cup Jerina offered him. "No, I want to—"

"Give that to Nattie, please, Paul," Jerina instructed. "And this one's for Chris."

Paul did as he was asked, then found Jerina's warm blue eyes smiling at him as she handed him his cup. That coming-home feeling prodded at him again. During the time he'd kept company with Chris, Jerina had fussed over and spoiled him, and eased the pervading loneliness caused by his mother's absence and his father's preoccupation with Eternity's single women. He'd learned to look after himself and to depend on no one. But Jerina had made him feel as though someone, besides Chris, cared.

He took the cup from her, wanting to do the honest thing, to set her and Nate straight about his situation with their daughter. But he couldn't do it.

She looked so pleased that he and Chris were married he simply couldn't step all over that with the truth. And her welcoming smile warmed him, enfolded him. Even after all these years, he felt himself responding to the comfort it provided.

"Thank you," he said, and folded himself onto the sofa beside Chris. She tucked her arm in his and squeezed cozily.

He made a private vow to swear off straight whiskeys for the rest of his life. Judging by the look on Nate's face, that could be counted in minutes.

Chapter Four

Chris and Paul, standing arm in arm on the front porch, waved as her parents drove away. The moment they were out of sight, Paul dropped his arm. "God, I didn't realize lying was so exhausting."

"There'll be time enough to explain when you leave," Chris said, turning to lean a hip against the porch railing. He was right. That had been a difficult hour and a half. "But for right now, this is the best thing to do if you don't want to lose your car."

He glanced at the sleek, silver Viper in the driveway, then back at her, his expression unreadable. "I'm surprised that that should concern you. Why didn't you tell your father that I don't remember a thing about last night?"

"Because I prefer to think that you do." She wrapped an arm around the turned support post and leaned her head against it. "I'd rather believe that you knew precisely what you were doing, just as I did."

"Maybe we should talk about that," he said, swinging a leg over the porch rail, leaving a foot's width between them. "This is going to be an awkward month if we don't."

She raised her head and turned to lean her back against the post. She folded her arms and studied him. "It's going to be an awkward month, anyway, if I want to be married and you don't."

"I mean, I think we should talk about the first time."

"The first wedding, you mean?" she asked in all apparent innocence. "I don't believe you can talk about it. You weren't there."

"I know," he said quietly. There were moments, in the endless hours of a sleepless night, when he would remember and find it impossible to believe he'd done that to her. He watched her eyes for some sign that he hadn't imagined the resentment in her voice—that she did hold him in contempt, and this was just an elaborate ruse to pay him back.

But her eyes were clear and looked directly into his. He braced himself and said, "I want to try to make you understand why I did that."

She shook her head. "It doesn't matter. You're here now."

"I'm not 'here,' Christy. And I'm not going to be—just as I wasn't the first time. There's a basic flaw in me that can't let me link with someone else."

She thought he was probably right, but she didn't think childhood trauma excused him. "I know," she said. "You hold a grudge against your father because his affairs drove your mom away. And I suppose you resent her because she left without you. I suppose when you love your parents and their marriage doesn't work, you come to believe marriage can't work for anybody. Am I close?"

He considered a moment. "Pretty close. And added to that, you were so absolutely sure of everything, so organized and systematic, and I felt so confined by my narrow little world."

She straightened in surprise. "You always told me you admired that about me."

He nodded. "I did. But the closer I came to promising my life to you, the more I began to realize that I didn't have what you needed."

"I adored you," she said, the words coming from her heart. For that instant, the plan was forgotten.

He smiled gently, affectionately, and she saw him exactly as he'd been at eighteen—without the big-city polish and the maturity of the added years.

"I know you did. But I didn't know what I felt. I began thinking about...The Plan—" he smiled again, capitalizing the words with his tone "—and realized I didn't know myself well enough to commit myself to it or to you. I felt, at that tender age, that everything I was, was defined by my loneliness. And I began to wonder if I loved you because I loved you, or because you loved me when my own family found it so easy to walk away from me."

Chris stared at him, trying to equate what he was telling her with the boy she'd known. "You did everything with such competence. You always seemed to know exactly what you were doing. You'd come to terms with your parents' divorce."

He swung his leg back over the railing onto the porch and stood. He turned to look out into the darkness. "I worked hard to give that impression. I didn't want anyone to suspect I was confused and uncertain."

"You used to tell *me* everything you felt," she reminded him softly, and with complete sincerity.

He turned to her with a look that, in the glare of the porch light, appeared indulgent. "You wanted me to be as sure of everything as you were, so I let you believe I was. I told you only what I knew you'd understand."

That hurt her. She struck back. "And you didn't think I'd understand if you told me you were going away, that I'd be left standing alone in the vestibule of the church waiting for you to show up?"

He was glad to see her display of temper. It made her seem real after all. Though she looked like the cool, new Christy persona, she was really the genuine original. He moved to stand inches away from her perch on the railing, his hands in the pockets of the dark pants he'd worn under the morning coat.

"I can't tell you how sorry I am that I did it that way. My only excuse is that I was young and stupid."

Chris's spine straightened a little further. "You're sorry you did it *that way,* but not that you did it?"

He shook his head, looking her directly in the eye. "I'm still convinced I did the best thing for both of us by not marrying you. You'd have taken charge of me and I'd have let you, because I had no idea where my life was going. I'd have fallen in with The Plan, and I'd have been absolutely no good for you."

She stood, too, feeling edgy and aggressive. How dared he mess with her clear memories of how things had been?

"What do you mean?"

"I mean," he said, reaching out to place a hand against the post behind her, just above her head, "you'd have turned into a bossy little matron who'd have organized our lives down to the last little detail. And I'd have let you, because at that time all I'd ever done was *react* to my life. I didn't know how to take charge of it." He tilted her face up and looked down into her eyes, his own dark in the shadow of the post. "You wouldn't be half as interesting as you've become."

Chris's thoughts were a muddle. And Paul's touch further distracted her from making any sense of them. She was beginning to wonder if they'd shared the same relationship.

"Maybe you were wrong," she suggested stiffly, "in sifting what you shared with me. Maybe I'd have understood more than you thought. Maybe I could have helped."

He opened his mouth as though to respond, then apparently changed his mind. He shook his head and leaned his shoulder against the post.

"The point I'm trying to make is that I know I did an unforgivable thing to you. And because of that, I don't understand why you married me last night."

Chris groped through her confusion for the threads of her scheme. "Because I've always wanted to marry you," she replied. Her voice was breathlessly convincing. That part was true. "And last night you made me believe that you've always wanted to marry me. How was I to know you lie when you're intoxicated?"

"I guess..." He paced across the porch, searching for an explanation. "I've always felt that I wanted to make it up to you. I suppose seeing you..." He turned from the other side of the steps, his eyes going over her with a troubled frown. "Seeing you brought back a lot of the old feelings. And you've matured into such a beautiful woman." He shrugged and walked slowly back to her. "I guess under the influence of too many straight shots of whiskey, I confused guilt with...love. I'm sorry."

She sighed and walked away from him, feeling strangely unlike herself. *You are playing a role,* she thought. *You don't mean half the things you're saying.* Yet, she had to admit that deep down, under layers of defensive emotion and years of self-delusion, a few things were very real.

Annoyed that this was becoming hard on her when it was supposed to hurt only him, she stood under the porch light and folded her arms, intent on finding a vulnerable point in him.

"I appreciate the apology," she said, "but hard as this is to admit, it was almost easier the first time, when you simply failed to show up." She yanked open the door. "But I'll stay out the month so that your friends will consider you deliriously happy and you'll get to keep your precious car. But as I warned you this morning, all's fair. For this month, you're mine, Bertrand. And I'm going to do everything in my power to make that permanent."

Paul shook his head at her. That statement brought the old Christy back into sharp focus. "You've never accepted the limits of any situation. You always had to push and pull until it came out your way."

"I know what I want," she said simply.

He closed the small distance between them. "If you haven't learned yet that you can't always have it, you haven't matured as much as I thought." He gestured her inside. "There's a bedroom across the hall from mine. I think you'll be comfortable there."

CHRIS DOUBTED she would be comfortable anywhere. She sat propped against the pillows in the darkness, a window open to let in the cold night air.

She was supposed to be in his arms tonight, driving him wild with desire. And here she was, relegated to the spare bedroom.

Bossy? She wasn't bossy. She was just sure of things, in charge, always formulating a plan. Only this time it was a scheme, and she was discovering that schemes had more dangerous elements than plans. Subterfuge and deceit had to be dealt with more carefully.

She frowned as she recalled Paul's saying she wouldn't be half as interesting as she'd become if he'd married her all those years ago. She tried to remember the young girl she'd been. When she thought back to that time, all she could usually remember was the pain of his defection. Now she tried to concentrate on the period before he left.

Love washed over her. She'd loved him so much. Her mind created an image of the Sussex River bridge and the kiss they'd shared there. He was tall and strong and she'd felt so protected in his arms. He'd fit every requirement of her young girl's dream.

She didn't want a knight in shining armor as most of her friends did. She wanted a newspaperman with his sleeves rolled up, a pencil behind his ear and a computer terminal humming to his righteous indignation over some injustice in his community.

Paul was perfect. He saw inside and under things, he understood what other boys didn't even consider twice, and he could explain it in simple words that packed enormous punch. And he liked her.

She'd developed The Plan and set out to implement it.

As the darkness hummed around her now, Chris thought about those words—and saw a new significance to them. She'd "set out to implement it."

It sounded a little cold-blooded. Yet that was the way she did everything. She'd develop a plan and carry it out. But at the riper age of almost thirty, she thought to question whether that was the right course to follow when another person's life and feelings were also involved.

She took one pillow out from behind her, tossed it aside, then slumped down into the other one. It wasn't as though she'd intended him any harm. She'd only wanted to love him, to share her life with him, to let him in on The Plan. Did that make her a bossy little matron?

As she closed her eyes, a quiet little voice inside her suggested, *Maybe he had plans of his own.*

She turned and pulled the pillow over her head.

PAUL WAS IN A CAGE. Both hands clenched on iron bars, feet braced against them, he pulled and cursed until the cage rattled and the air was blue with his fury. He finally fell to the floor on his back, exhausted.

Then he turned to sit up and noticed that the door was open. He stared at the path to freedom in amazement. A woman wearing a white dress and a veil moved to stand in the opening. She placed a hand to each side of the doorframe, blocking his way. It was Christy.

"Paul," she said softly.

He backed away from her.

"Paul," she said more loudly, reaching out a hand for him.

"Stay away from me!" he shouted at her.

"Paul!" A quiet but firm voice penetrated Paul's dream and brought him to the edge of consciousness.

He struggled before surrendering to complete wakefulness. One of his hands held his pillow and the other lay across his stomach. And there was no weight against him but the cotton of his shorts. Satisfied that he was alone in bed, he opened his eyes.

Chris stood over him in a prim blue dress that buttoned down the front and flared at her knees. "Don't worry," she said. "I'm not trying to get into bed with you. I'm just trying to get you out of it." As she spoke, she yanked the covers off him. "Church services are in twenty minutes. I took Louis his breakfast and he's waiting for you to help him down the stairs. Come on. I'm always at services and so are several of your friends. They'll expect to see you."

She faltered as her deft yank revealed six foot something of naked male, except for the strip of taut cotton across his hips that concealed very little.

Their relationship as teenagers had never graduated to the removal of clothing, but she doubted he'd have looked anything like this as a boy. Every muscled contour of his chest, the lean indentation of his stomach and the long, corded length of thigh and femur said "man." She was sure that definition would have been punctuated by what the cotton covered, but she resolutely ignored it.

Her gaze reached his eyes and she found that he was leaning up on an elbow and grinning at her perusal of his charms.

"I'm not sure you should go to church," he teased, "with that look on your face."

She would not let him put her off-balance again today. "I was simply admiring God's beautiful design," she said, meeting his gaze without wavering.

"Your cheeks are pink."

"I'll look like a blushing bride. Now, are you getting up, or do I have to get rough?"

He considered her without moving, his eyes lively with interest. "Let me think about that. What would 'getting rough' involve exactly?"

She folded her arms. "Cold water poured on you."

He raised an eyebrow. "Think you could accomplish that without getting roughed up yourself?"

The interest in his eyes had deepened to something far more dangerous. She continued to hold his gaze, but she shifted her weight and fidgeted.

"Absolutely. I have several karate classes and three years of aerobics under my belt."

In a movement so swift Chris didn't see it coming, Paul snagged her wrist, yanked her onto him, then turned and pinned her to the sheet.

She was surprised to find that she was literally trapped. She could not move. The top of her dress had unbuttoned, and his naked leg pinned hers to the mattress. Since her skirt was somewhere around her waist she could feel his warm thigh through her panty hose.

His dark gaze ran slowly over her flustered features, studied her lips for a long, unnerving moment, then went to her wide eyes. "You shouldn't threaten an opponent," he said softly, "until you're sure you're not outclassed. I was the *Globe*'s entry three years in

a row in the All Boston Amateur Boxing competi
tion. Took first place twice."

She tried to move a hand, a leg, anything. But she
was completely immobile. So she asked, "What hap
pened the third time?"

He grinned. "I was mugged by two guys on my way
to the arena. Held 'em both till the police arrived. I go
there too late to compete."

Then he pushed away from her and strode to the
doorway. "But I guess we'll have to explore this an
other time. Wouldn't want you to be late for church."

THE PASTOR, a tall, spare man with graying brown
hair, hugged Chris, then shook Paul's hand enthusi
astically. "Congratulations, you two!" he said as his
congregation streamed past him down the steps. "
was delighted to hear the news, though I'm disap
pointed you didn't let me perform the wedding
Bronwyn allows me to use the chapel, you know."

Chris nodded apologetically. "It was the middle o
the night, and Bronwyn happened to be up. But we're
pleased to have your blessing."

The pastor turned to Paul's father, balanced be
hind them on his crutches. "Good to see you, Louis
Been a while since you've visited."

Louis pointed at Paul with his crutch. "I have seri
ous things to pray for now—and to be thankful for."

The pastor put a paternal hand on his shoulder
"Don't forget to pray for yourself," he said.

"Wonderful sermon, Pastor." They were joined by
Carlotta Ormsby, who'd driven Louis to the wedding
the day before. She tucked a companionable arm in
Louis's, despite the crutch.

"You know," she said, smiling at Chris and Paul, "I was wondering. I have a room to let, and I think Louis would be very comfortable in it. It'd allow you two to have privacy, and I'd have ready access to my favorite Scrabble partner."

"Ready access?" Pastor Bue repeated in concern.

Carlotta smiled angelically. "Oh, Louis and I have been friends for years." As though that revelation should cancel any notion of impropriety, she turned to Chris and Paul. "You shouldn't have to start your married lives having to look after an invalid. Let me look after him, at least for a couple of weeks. Then we can reassess. If he's miserable with me, at least you two will have had a little time together."

Louis huffed in good-natured protest. "Do I look like an invalid?"

"Yes," she replied frankly. "You look like an invalid on crutches. And I was a nurse before I married Wallace Ormsby. You'll be in good hands."

"But, Louis has been no trouble," Chris insisted, looking to Paul for support. "We're happy to—"

"I think it's a good idea," Louis interrupted. He met his son's eyes and asked, as though it really mattered to him, "What do you think, Paul?"

Paul took a moment to answer. His father was expecting him to encourage him to go. He wasn't sure if he resisted doing the expected out of perversity or if he was getting soft.

"I think," he finally replied, "that Chris and I are living in your house, where you're perfectly welcome to stay. But I also think you should do what makes you most comfortable."

Louis's eyes held his for a long moment, and for just an instant, Paul felt that unsettling coming-home feeling again. He remembered that look from very early in his childhood, when things had been good between his parents and everyone had been happy. He'd almost forgotten that he and Louis had once connected very well—that they'd loved each other.

Louis turned to give the widow a high-wattage smile. "Thank you, Carlotta. I accept your generous invitation."

"Good. Shall we stop by the house for your things?"

"Maybe Chris and Paul would bring them by later?"

Chris nodded. "Of course."

"Have a wonderful Sunday, all of you." Carlotta smiled glowingly at the newlyweds and the pastor. "Come along, Louis. Mind the stairs. I have a pot roast in the oven, and I'm making candied parsnips just the way you..." Her voice faded away as Louis reached the bottom of the steps and she gently took his arm and slowly led the way to a shiny white Lincoln.

The pastor looked after them worriedly.

Chris looked up at Paul, unable to withhold a grin. The hand he'd placed around her shoulders for the pastor's benefit now squeezed gently as he shared the moment. Her heart reacted as though she'd been kissed.

A cluster of little children gathered around the pastor, and Chris took advantage of the moment to bid him good-day and encourage Paul down the steps. They'd brought her car to accommodate Louis's crutches. She breathed a sigh of relief as she looked in a small black shoulder bag for her keys.

"What is it about clergymen," she asked, "that makes you feel as though they see right through you?"

Paul laughed, took the keys from her and opened the passenger door. "I think he does see through my father. He looked pretty concerned for Carlotta's moral well-being."

"Good heavens, your father's in a cast."

Paul raised an eyebrow. "It is possible to make love to a woman while in a cast."

She faced him, hands on her hips. "I'm sure you know this from experience."

"Yes," he admitted, shooing her into the car. When she tried to take the keys from him, he held them away. "I'm driving because I'm taking you someplace special for breakfast."

"All right." She slipped into the seat, remembering that her father had always praised Paul's safe, sane driving. Of course, he hadn't known what went on in the hills around town on weekends, and she hadn't enlightened him. Still, curiously, she trusted Paul implicitly with anything she owned—except her heart.

Needing to clear her mind of that thought, she said as she belted herself in, "I want to hear about how you researched that fact about making love while in a cast."

He secured his seat belt and put the key in the ignition. "It involved an overturned jeep in Saudi Arabia, a U.S. Army nurse and the night she was off duty." He turned on the engine and pulled at his tie. "But I'm more interested in what's happening right now. Ready?"

"Ready."

It took her all of five minutes to realize where he was taking her—mostly because it only required five minutes to cross Eternity from border to border. The

Peabody was half a mile out of town and still the best place on the Eastern seaboard to buy crab rolls.

Chris was surprised by this nostalgic action on his part. In the old days, they'd always ended up at the Peabody after late nights working on the school paper, going to sports events, dances or movies. Even when they'd been broke, they'd shared a shake and an order of onion rings.

Chris glanced at her watch, trying not to look as pleased as she felt. "Onion rings for breakfast?"

He turned into the lot, which was already half-full. "It's almost eleven and I've been dreaming about the crab rolls since I got here. A side of fries, maybe a side of onion rings, and I'll be a happy man."

She watched him set the brake. "Somehow," she said, "I thought it would take more than that."

PAUL PACKED a box of clothes and personal items he thought his father would need. As an afterthought, he threw in the bag of limes. Then he delivered the lot to Carlotta Ormsby's.

She lived in a contemporary stone-and-glass house set in the middle of a cluster of pines at the west end of Eternity. She directed him to his father, seated in a recliner before an entertainment center that took up an entire wall.

A plaid blanket covered his knees, and at his right hand was a small table bearing a pedestal glass filled with what appeared to be coffee topped by a dollop of cream. Beside it was a thick slice of a spice cake he'd caught a whiff of from the edge of the room.

Carlotta capably took the box from him and nudged him farther into the room. "I'll put this away. Go on in and say hi. I'll bring you a cup of coffee and a piece of cake."

"Thank you," he said, "but I just finished breakfast."

"Just coffee, then?"

"Thanks, but I'm stuffed."

She nodded, her smile knowing. "Anxious to get back to Chris, aren't you?" With that, she disappeared down a corridor.

Louis looked up, then immediately clicked off the movie he'd been watching. He smiled hesitantly at Paul. "Everything all right?"

Paul went into the room and took a Boston rocker placed at a right angle to his father's chair. "Yeah. I just brought you some clothes, your shaving gear, a few things I thought you'd need."

Paul nodded gratefully. "I appreciate it. Carlotta's made me very comfortable, as you can see." He grinned. "I may just take a permanent lease on this chair. You adjusting to married life?"

"I think I can last the month."

Louis sobered. "How's Chris taking it? Friday night, she thought you knew what you were doing, that you wanted to marry her."

Paul studied the view from the window. "She's convinced she can change my mind."

"She's a very beautiful woman."

"She is," Paul agreed, getting restlessly out of the chair. "Women have their place, but not in my life. The desperate need to be cosseted by one is not something I inherited from you."

"Yes, you did," Louis replied calmly. "Every man who's ever loved a woman will always need one. You may deny it, you may suppress it, but nothing in your life will ever replace the spiritual and physical experience of a loving woman's arms around you."

Paul, halfway to the window, stopped and turned. The look he gave Louis made him expel a sigh and lean back in his chair.

"And that's so essential to you that, even while you had Mom's arms around you, you had to fill the moments you were apart from her in another woman's arms? And another?" He looked around him at the comfortable surroundings. "Even approaching seventy, that's still a strong influence in your life, isn't it?"

"Carlotta made the offer out of kindness," Louis said, his eyes darkening. "Nothing else."

Paul jammed his hands into his pockets and nodded. "I don't doubt that for a moment. I only question why you accepted."

Louis frowned at him in confusion. "So that you and Chris could be alone. This morning, you weren't against my coming here."

Paul noticed Carlotta in the doorway. He closed his eyes, wondering why the hell he was picking a fight in someone else's home. "Yeah, well, Mom wasn't part of it then."

"Your mother *isn't* part of it," Louis said, his voice low and tight. "She left us, remember?"

"Yes." Paul glared at him one last moment. "I also remember why." With an apologetic glance at Carlotta, he left the room and let himself out of the house.

Carlotta went to stand behind Louis's chair. She rested a hand on his shoulder and patted gently. "Why didn't you say something?" she asked.

Louis groaned softly. "Because it isn't time. He has other things to settle first."

"You might leave it too late."

"No," he said firmly. "I won't."

Chapter Five

Paul was edgy with anger and confusion. He was angry because he thought he'd put all that behind him. Hell, he was a big-time journalist with almost celebrity status. Why did he still feel that gut-wrenching emptiness he'd known when his mother had left?

He could see her now in his mind's eye, sitting on his bed in a bright yellow sundress, telling him tearfully that she had to leave and she couldn't take him with her.

Confused by her distress, missing the enormity of her statement, he'd asked her when she was coming back. She'd burst into sobs, hugged him, then composed herself and told him, "Never. But you'll come and see me."

But that had never come to pass. A letter had explained that she'd moved to Europe. There'd been postcards, gifts, a generous check when he'd graduated from high school. Years later, just before his graduation from college, a telegram from her attorney had informed him that she'd died after a brief illness. There was no estate, no personal effects other than clothing, which she'd asked be given to a friend.

And so she'd gone out of his life even more completely than she had when he'd been eleven. That gnawing hole had opened up in him, and he'd closed it by joining friends in a scull race on the Charles River, then in a whiskey race at a local pub. He'd awakened twenty-five hours later, in physical agony, but emotionally purged—he'd thought.

And here it was again. As gaping and painful as it had been then.

Paul stormed up the steps of the old house where he'd been raised and barged through the door, grateful Christy wasn't there to greet him. He marched into his bedroom, pulling at his tie as he went, yanking at the buttons of his shirt.

He hated the confusion as much as the anger. He didn't want to care about Louis. Even as a child of eleven, he'd heard the gossip. His father's affair with a local woman had driven his mother away.

He rid himself of his suit pants and pulled on his old jeans.

Everyone had talked about it. He remembered his father in those days, tall and slender and unfailingly good-natured. He recalled clearly a confrontation with him one evening after dinner, the abuse he'd heaped on him for ruining his life. Louis had simply put an arm around him and tried to speak calmly.

But the boy he'd been wasn't all that different from the man he'd become. He'd analyzed the situation according to the information he'd learned, according to the burning pain he felt, and reached his own conclusions. Then he'd spoken them plainly and concisely.

"I hate you. I'll live with you because I have to. But the moment I graduate, I'm out of here."

Paul reached into the bottom of his closet for the ragged Boston College sweatshirt in which he met all his crises. It wasn't there. He got down on his knees to root through the rubble of shoes, laundry, things that had fallen off hangers when he'd pulled other things out of the closet.

He remembered that Louis had accepted his withdrawal, then fought it subtly for seven years. But during that time there'd been a succession of other women in his life, and Paul, the judge, had kept his distance.

Where was the damn shirt? He pushed to his feet, checked through the pajamas he'd left on the chair, then yanked the hem of the bedspread up to look under it. Someone, he noticed absently, had made the bed.

He found a paperback he'd been reading several days ago and lost, a crumpled T-shirt and his disreputable Rockports. He removed his dress shoes, sat on the edge of the bed and pulled on his running shoes.

He remembered the insidious feeling that had lingered in Paul, the boy, and seemed to be with him still. That deeply ingrained physical memory of Louis holding him as a toddler, running with him as he learned to ride his bike, comforting him when Joshua Baldwin blackened his eye in the school yard, then signing him up for boxing lessons at the Y. He remembered being loved.

He turned away from that thought, wishing he could remember what the hell he'd done with his sweatshirt. He went to the hamper in the bathroom and lifted the lid. Empty. He checked the hook on the back of the bathroom door. Nope.

Going back into the bedroom, he yanked a pink-and-purple-plaid flannel shirt his friends had teased him about out of the closet and pulled it on.

Well, there had to be more to loving than strong arms and seeing that your son was taught the manly art of self-defense. There had to be a certain ethical code upheld. If a man loved his son, he shouldn't cheat on the boy's mother. Paul had held to that law as a child, and he held to it now.

He went downstairs, spoiling for trouble.

Halfway down, he noticed that the living room had been tidied. Christy's bentwood rocker had been placed near the fireplace, along with an old wooden bucket that held a mass of weedy-looking things.

The love seat had been set against the entrance to the hallway, and behind it was the high skinny table. On it was the old graniteware canner that had been abandoned in the kitchen cupboard when he and his father had moved in. It, too, was full of weeds.

The draperies were open, and sharp, early-autumn sunlight poured through the sheers. The effect softened his mood. He didn't want it to, resisted it the rest of the way down the stairs. Then he became aware of the wonderful aroma filling the house. Beef and vegetables, if he wasn't mistaken. He walked into the kitchen to find a pot roast in the oven. The aroma wound around him, softening his mood further. Carlotta had been fixing pot roast. He wondered if everyone in Eternity was having pot roast for dinner.

But where was Christy? He peered through the curtained window on the back door and had his answer. She sat in the middle of the backyard surrounded by four bales of hay and what appeared to be a pile of laundry. On one of the bales sat the black cat from next door, leaning precariously forward into Christy's work like a vulture. As he watched, she reached out to pet the cat. The animal arched under Christy's hand, long, pliant tail going straight up as she leaned into her touch.

Something curious and unidentifiable took place in Paul's chest. But he'd had enough confusion for one day. He opened the door and walked down the back porch steps to join her.

Paul sat on one of the bales as Christy squinted over at him. She, too, had changed into jeans, topping them with a worn red sweater. Her hair was woven into one long braid that she'd secured at the end with a plain rubber band. The braid shone in the sunlight like a hank of some magically spun thread.

"Your father comfortable?" she asked.

He didn't want to think about his father anymore this afternoon. He nodded casually and reached out to stroke the cat. "He's fine. I see you've met Morticia."

She smiled at the cat, then turned back to a pair of brown pants in her lap and a clump of hay. As she held the pants up to stuff in more hay, he could see that she'd already filled the legs and was working on the seat.

"Morticia's been offering advice. She thinks this one should be fat."

Paul frowned at her. "This...scarecrow? Has it escaped your notice that we don't have a garden?"

"These are decorative, not functional scarecrows. He's for the front porch. That one—" she pointed behind the bale on which he sat "—is for the bench in front of the shop."

Paul followed her pointing finger.

"So there's my sweatshirt," he said, surprised to find himself more amused than annoyed that she'd taken it. A good four inches of the maroon-and-gold fleece was torn away from the ribbed neckline, there was a large hole in one elbow, and the barn red paint the Beautiful Boston protesters had been using to make placards lay in an artful swath across the lower half.

Chris looked up in alarm. "You mean you still wear it? I was cleaning up our...your room and found it in the bottom of the closet next to your shoeshine stuff. I thought it was a rag."

He pretended indignation as he pulled the thin scarecrow off the grass and stood it before him to eye it critically. It wore rather small gray sweats, his maroon-and-gold shirt, a face made of plain white fabric on which she'd painted big eyes and a wide smile. On its squarish head was a Red Sox baseball cap.

"I beg your pardon," he said, leaning the figure against his hay bale. "That is not a rag. That's the shirt in which I bench pressed 350 pounds, trained for the All Boston Amateur Boxing championship, interviewed William F. Buckley when I found him sitting in Boston Common and helped my buddies win a rowing regatta on the Charles River."

She looked doubtfully from him to the shirt, then back to him again. "I apologize," she said finally. "I suppose if you weren't already determined to leave me, this would be grounds for divorce."

There was no whine and no condemnation in her tone—just a sort of fatalistic acceptance. And she gave him a wry grin, rather than a martyred look. Given the way he'd felt when he'd arrived home from Carlotta's, he was grateful. Grateful enough to fold up onto the grass beside her and offer to help. "Anything I can do?"

Chris played it cool. Not just because she didn't want him to see in her eyes that she considered his amenability a small success for her side, but because her own feelings were growing too warm to do otherwise.

His shoulder bumped hers, his after-shave mingled with the wonderful pungency of autumn and wood smoke, and his large hands, taking a pile of clothing from her, looked strong and supple, as she knew they were.

Some kind of tumult had gone on in him today, she knew. She could see it in his eyes. She guessed it was related to his visit to his father. She was glad she'd decided to appeal to that part of every man that couldn't help but appreciate a cozy home and an aromatic meal cooking—even if he didn't think he wanted those things.

The schemer in her laughed at herself for caring. The woman... the woman was confused.

"Ah." Paul held up the stockings and skirt she handed him. "I'm making a girl?"

She smiled, surprised by his hesitation. "Yes. Are you afraid she'll get you drunk and marry you when you're not looking?"

He gave her a quick scolding look, then turned his eyes back to the stockings he held up.

She took the stockings and the skirt from him and handed him the topless male scarecrow. "Here. Finish him. But I find it hard to believe you're paralyzed by a woman's underclothing."

"I've removed a woman's clothing," he admitted. "But I've never put her back into them."

She indicated the torn flannel shirt she'd given him. "Just stuff the shirt." She grinned. "That's something you should be good at."

It was a moment before he got the joke. Then he dropped a handful of hay into her hair.

CHATEAUBRIAND, Paul decided, could not have been more delicious than Chris's pot roast and vegetables. The meal was accompanied by light flaky biscuits and her outstanding coffee.

"I don't remember that you had great culinary skills as a girl," he said, buttering a halved biscuit. "Where did this come from?"

She shrugged. "I guess it was a natural skill I never had the opportunity to indulge." She put a dollop of horseradish on the side of her plate and passed him the pottery jar. "When I came home from college and before I opened the shop, weekends were kind of long, so I experimented with cooking and had everyone I knew over for dinner."

Weekends were kind of long. Paul imagined her, a beautiful, lonely young woman bumping around an empty apartment, filling her time by learning to cook.

"I was working for the *Blue News* in those days," he said reflectively. "A poorman's version of *Variety*. Real poor. I covered every music and theater event within a hundred miles of Boston while trying to get on at the *Globe.*"

"What made them finally hire you?"

He shook his head at his own impudence. "I was playing pickup football with some friends on Boston Common and William F. Buckley was sitting on a bench."

"Ah," she said. "And you were wearing your Boston College sweatshirt, so you felt invincible."

"Right. He gave me an interview, I took it to the city editor I'd been haranguing day and night to give me a chance—and he did. I did city news for a year, then they sent me to cover Andrei Sakharov's return to Moscow when Gorbachev declared glasnost. And I've been traveling ever since."

"So you had too much to do to be lonely."

He was quiet a moment as he considered. Then he said finally, looking at her, "I've felt lonely most of my life. Except for the Christy years."

She straightened in surprise. "The what?"

"The Christy years," he repeated, smiling quietly in self-deprecation. "That's how I always think of it. I was close to my parents before the divorce, but from the day my mother left, I never got close to anyone—except you."

She was stunned to hear him admit it. For an instant she wanted to push him the rest of the way, to make him admit that he regretted what he'd done, not just the hurting her, but the leaving. But he moved his plate aside, folded his arms on the table and disarmed her completely by saying, "Tell me. How *was* our wedding night?"

A major fluster rose immediately to bring a blush to her cheeks and a stammer to her lips. She kept them closed until her thoughts fell into order.

"I told you yesterday morning," she reminded him with a shy glance away that was not entirely feigned, "that you were superb."

He looked suspicious. "I find that hard to believe, considering I was too intoxicated to remember marrying you."

"Maybe," she said, "it's because making sense and making love require very different responses."

He acknowledged the truth of that with a light laugh. Then he reached a hand across the small kitchen table to cover hers, his expression growing serious. "I used to dream about making love to you all the time in the old days," he said. "I hate knowing that I missed it, or that I might not have cherished you as I'd always planned to do when I finally brought you to my bed."

His concern was so sincere that Chris was the one who felt guilty. Appalled that that should happen, she reminded herself heartlessly that this was all part of the scheme. Then she covered his hand with her free one and stroked it gently.

"Maybe one day," she said, looking into his eyes, "we'll try it again when you know what you're doing." Then she pulled her plate to her and casually began to catch him up on their old friends.

Chris saw his eyes wander over her, his mind attentive but his sexual interest speculating. She felt a small thrill of victory. The scheme was beginning to work. She just had to be careful not to overplay.

"WOULD YOU LIKE breakfast before I go?"

Paul, already awake, turned his gaze from the window to the doorway of his bedroom where Chris stood in gray leggings and a color-blocked, oversize pullover in shades of teal, fuchsia and yellow. Her hair was down, and she was fiddling with an earring.

He felt a startling sense of desire he didn't understand. The outfit was chic but not particularly sexy, except maybe in the way the pants clung to her legs.

Maybe it was her hair, loose and gleaming. Or the very basic wifely question she'd asked.

He sat up, frowning at her. "I thought the nineties male fended for himself domestically, because his wife's usually busier than he is."

Her earring in place, she put a hand on either side of the doorway and leaned in to smile at him. "In Boston, maybe. In Eternity, where marriage lasts forever, we're always attentive to each other's needs. You're my husband. I'd never leave you without breakfast when I have to prepare my own. It's the little things that make love a wheel."

"A wheel?"

"Never ending, always turning."

After so many years studying and reporting the seamy underbelly of an increasingly cruel world, Paul felt as though he'd dropped into some parallel universe where things were sweeter, more beautiful, softer.

"Thank you," he said. "But I have to run some errands. I'll get breakfast while I'm out."

She smiled and blew him a kiss. "Okay. Have a good day."

"Christy."

She was already halfway down the hallway. He heard the click of her low heels on the hardwood floor as she returned. Only her head reappeared, her hair raining down as she tilted it to look into the room. "Yeah?"

"You'd see that I got breakfast," he said, his tone faintly injured, "but you'd go off without kissing me goodbye?"

She looked at him in surprise for a moment, then that turned to smiling suspicion. "You led me to believe you don't want that kind of thing between us."

"You led me to believe you'd do everything in your power to change my mind."

He was asking for it, in more ways than one. Chris understood her priorities this morning. The scheme was in good order, and she had herself under control. There was no reason to feel sorry for him, to reevaluate her strategy. If he did have fond memories of her, if he was lonely, he had only himself to blame.

Her perfect center wavered a little as she approached the bed. Paul's hair was tousled, his eyes were like a moonless midnight, and he had a sexy night's growth of beard Don Johnson would have envied. She placed a tight rein on herself.

"So I did," she said as she approached the bed.

Expecting him to remain in it, she was surprised when he rose up out of it, bracing one foot on the floor, the other bent among the covers as he reached for her. She caught a quick glimpse of those damnable cotton briefs before his mouth closed over hers.

It was not a goodbye kiss. It represented instead everything she'd hoped to arouse in him—fascination, desire and a suggestion of desperation. It was in the hands that gripped her arms and lifted her on tiptoe, in the lips that started at her mouth, worked over her jaw, her ear, her neck, and ended finally in her hair.

She managed to maintain her equanimity until he wound one arm around her and tilted her head back with the other. His eyes were filled with everything she'd felt in him, and a smoky tenderness that lay over it all.

She felt that pinch of guilt again and pushed away from him with sudden firmness. She realized her mistake too late. He was studying her with perplexity.

"Gotta run," she said, straining on tiptoe again to give him a resounding kiss on his cheek. "Have a good day. If you have any spare time this afternoon, I have a shipment coming you could help me with."

"What time?"

"Anytime after lunch. No hurry. 'Bye."

Good save, Chris congratulated herself as she ran down the stairs to the front door. You got away, but you invited him to the store. He has to be convinced that you didn't pull away from him, but that you simply had to hurry.

Close, girl.

Upstairs, Paul frowned on his way to the shower. She'd responded as though she'd cared, then she'd pushed him away. Didn't take a genius to figure that out, he told himself. The chemistry was still there, would probably always be there. But he'd hurt her and, even though she'd married him, that was bound to hit her in the face now and then.

And it wasn't as if this was going to be permanent, as if he'd have to understand every little move she made, every little shadow in her eyes. In a month, he'd be on his way back to Boston in the Viper.

He stepped into the shower, adjusted the water and let it hit him full force. He had the damnedest feeling he was feeding himself a crock. His situation—and his woman—were more complicated than they appeared. Every investigative instinct he possessed told him so.

"ARE YOU GOING to buy the *Courier* like you'd always planned?" Erica's eyes glowed as she followed

Chris around the store while she replenished stock. "Are you going to the Bahamas on your fifth anniversary, then have half a dozen babies? Tell me. Tell me *everything*."

Chris tucked the last pocket-tissue package into the rack of travel essentials and straightened to look at her assistant and young friend. Erica's eyes were bright with curiosity, her expression soft with the happily-ever-after syndrome she was still young enough to believe in.

Chris tapped the stack of books Erica held to her chest. "What are you doing here on your day off? Shouldn't you be home putting that Senior Issues paper together?"

Erica followed Chris to the counter. "This is research. Love and romance qualify as senior issues. What's he like? Is he as totally cool as he looks?"

Chris scooped up an armful of body lotions and arranged them neatly on a tall glass shelf near the front door. She scanned the shelf, noted which soaps were low and went back to the stack of freight boxes behind the counter to search for them. It was easier to lie to Erica with her face hidden behind the flaps of a carton.

"There's not much to tell. He's pretty much the same as I remember."

"You loved him all these years," Erica said breathlessly, "and he came back to you." She closed her eyes and squeezed her books to her. "It's just *too* much!"

This conversation is becoming too much, Chris thought, moving a box of tote bags and matching sun shades aside to search the box underneath. Lying to anyone was difficult—and rapidly becoming a distasteful part of the scheme. But lying to the girl who

idolized and believed in her ranked right up there with
lying to her parents.

"I can't *wait* to marry Alex." Erica put her books
down on the counter and reached for the box knife.
She handed it to Chris, who struggled with the lids of
a deep narrow carton that looked promising.

"Has he given up on the idea of a scholarship?"

"Yeah. He's got a three-point-five average, and
most of the other candidates are four-point. And I'm
sure whoever decides these things won't care that he'd
have done better if he hadn't worked thirty hours a
week the last two years of school."

"Maybe something great will happen, anyway."

"That's what your husband told him at the wedding. He's trying to believe it, but he knows it won't
happen. So we'll just both get jobs after school, get
married, and later, when we've got money, I'll put him
through myself."

"I don't know, Erica," Chris said, trying not to
sound like a wet blanket. "The things you put off until after marriage never get done. Before you know it,
you have babies and mortgages. Aha! Soap!"

Erica reached down to help her lift the box onto the
counter. She followed Chris with her hands full of tis-
sue-wrapped herbal soaps back to the tall shelf. "I'll
find a way. You know how I am when I make up my
mind."

Chris had to smile at her. She did. This was the same
girl who brought the Eternity High volleyball team to
the state finals with a sprained knee and a contact lens
lost somewhere on the court. She could manage the
shop by herself on a Saturday, handle difficult customers with adultlike poise, and she held the record

for the most fund-raising chocolate bars sold for the school in the past ten years.

Chris felt proud of her, and also felt an unsettling sense of déjà vu. At Erica's tender age, she still thought anything she wanted could be brought about by force of will and determination. She was too young to know that attitude worked with things, but not necessarily with people. But Chris didn't want to rain on her parade. That was bound to happen somewhere down the road. Let someone else do it.

"You still planning to make your wedding dress?" The fragrances of the soaps wafted up around them, making the shop smell like forests and wildflowers.

"I'm collecting ideas. I *have* to show you what I cut out of *Bride and Beauty.* They're so chic. Only trouble is I'll have to have four weddings to use all the ideas."

Soaps in place, unopened boxes abandoned, they leaned over the counter while Erica showed Chris her collection of clippings. Chris noted with a private smile that they'd been collected in a folder labeled Mrs. Alex Powell.

"I like the sleeves on this one, but the bodice on this one. And *look* at this train. Isn't that gorgeous?"

It was cathedral length. Chris duly admired it. "But you'd have to take out a loan just to buy enough fabric for that. And how would you work on half a mile of satin in that little corner of your bedroom where the sewing machine is?"

Erica gave her an indulgently disgruntled look. "You sound like Mom. For every idea I have, she has six reasons why it won't work. I'll spread the fabric out over the bed. It'll be easy." She rooted through the clippings with a frown of concentration. "Here it is. Look at this beading! Isn't that elegant?"

"Erica, that would take you five months just to—" Chris looked up into Erica's frown and stopped herself. "It's beautiful. I love it. Show me what to do and I'll help you bead. If we hire an army of couturiers, we can be done by next fall."

Erica leaned against her, giggling, and that set Chris off. She needed very much to laugh. Life had gotten rather serious somehow since the initiation of the scheme.

"Well, well." Chris looked up from the clippings into Paul's amused dark eyes. He was leaning on his elbows on the other side of the counter. Their faces were inches apart. Her skin prickled with sexual awareness. She thought he noted that before he turned to her assistant with a devastating smile. "Hi, Erica. I thought you were off today."

Erica beamed into his eyes. "I was. I just came to hear all about you."

He raised an eyebrow, his gaze swinging back to Chris. "What did you hear?"

Erica shook her head in dramatic disappointment. "Not much. Chris won't talk. But she doesn't really have to. Whenever I mention you, she gets this look in her eyes and this kind of glow."

"Really." Paul searched Chris's face, apparently looking for those reactions. Chris straightened away from him, sure he'd find them if he was allowed to search hard enough.

"I'd better go." Erica cast Chris a very unsubtle wink, reassembled her folder and gathered up her books. "See you tomorrow afternoon, Chris. 'Bye, Mr. Bertrand."

"'Bye, Erica."

When the door closed behind the girl, Paul braced his hands on the counter and leaned toward Chris, his eyes alight with mischief. "So, what'd you say about me?"

Refusing to succumb to his wicked charm when she had her own agenda, Chris braced her fingertips and leaned toward him until their lips were only a breath apart.

"That our destiny finally came to pass. That you're everything I've ever dreamed of and more than worth the wait."

The mischief in his eyes wavered and he scolded, "You lied to her."

"No, I didn't," she said softly. "I was judging by the night you unfortunately don't remember."

He didn't give a damn what she was judging by. All his mind could comprehend was that her eyes were wide and filled with pleasure as they roved over his face, that her skin did glow as Erica said, and her lips were parted in expectation.

Chris forgot for a moment what she was doing. His face was like an up-close ad for men's cologne. It filled her vision and her consciousness. She saw fathomless dark eyes under thick, neatly drawn brows. The strong contours of his face were now cleanly shaven, and his lips... She remembered what they felt and tasted like—warm, mobile, confident.

The memory became reality when he tilted his head and closed the small gap between them. His mouth closed over hers—and instantly erased any relation this had to previous kisses. He teased her for a moment with light touches, little nibbles and a dip of his tongue that made her gasp and shiver in reaction.

Wanting more than the merciless little taunts, she reached both hands behind his head and explored his lips with the tip of her tongue. Then she ventured inside and used every wile in her meager store.

Paul felt her response down at the heart of his masculinity, and experienced a subtle but absolute change within himself. He lifted her onto the counter, swung her legs toward and around him, then placed his hands under her hips and pulled her to him.

That subtle change telegraphed itself to Chris. It was on his lips and in his touch. Possession. The thrill of it filled every little corner of her being.

"Well." A masculine voice brought Chris's head up. Paul continued to nibble at her throat. In the open doorway, she saw a handsome, middle-aged couple, hand in hand. He wore a boutonniere, and she wore a blue silk suit and a sparkling smile.

Chris smiled back, knowing they'd just come from the chapel.

The man indicated their intimate position with a gesture of his free hand. "I guess you're proof that the products in here are guaranteed."

The couple disappeared, laughing, down an aisle.

Chris cleared her throat, having a little difficulty fighting her way out of the rosy little haze Paul had created around her. "I asked you to come," she said in a businesslike tone that had a very ineffective note of censure in it, "to help me with the freight."

He smiled with complete lack of contrition, pulling her even closer. "That's always been the problem with us. I have my own plans. You just never notice them when you're going about yours."

He pulled her head down to kiss her again, then lifted her off the counter. "Okay. Where is it, and what do you want me to do with it?"

As Chris pointed out the cartons filled with heavy goods she wanted moved to the back of the shop, she reminded herself to be cautious. She couldn't afford to entangle the scheme with old emotions and dreams.

But when he gave her a look that promised something undefined at the moment, she realized that her cautions were worthless. She watched him walk away, effortlessly carrying a large box of books, broad back and lean hips moving with easy grace, and could wonder only what her wedding night would have been like had it really happened.

Chapter Six

"Shall I take you out to dinner?" Paul locked the shop door and turned the Open sign to Closed while Chris counted cash.

She stuffed the bank deposit into the zippered bag. "We have leftover pot roast."

"I made a sandwich for lunch." He wandered up and down aisles, pulling things off the shelves, studying them, then putting them back. "I'll have the rest tomorrow. Does the Bridge Street Café still make the best pizza east of the Rockies?"

"Absolutely," she said, zipping the bag and tossing it onto her purse. She delved into a shelf under the counter for a new roll of register tape. "Do you still pick off the olives?"

He looked up from a bottle of massage oil to grin at her. "No, because I order it without. Don't tell me you still get the 'deadly combination.'"

"Every time."

"Then I guess I'll be picking off the olives. Do people really fall for this stuff?"

Chris slipped the tape onto the bar, then looked up at him with a frown. "What do you mean 'fall for this stuff'?"

"Well—" he wandered toward her as he read from the label "—'Heaven Oil rubbed gently on the body from neck to toes will guarantee a night you'll remember. Smooth on our magic mixture and feel the sensuous heavens open and...'" He stopped with a roll of his eyes. "Come on. Like an oil could do that."

"I can't keep it in stock. Locals buy it again and again."

He turned back to replace it on the shelf. "You're smart, of course, to stock what sells. It just amazes me that people believe a honeymoon—or any night—will be enhanced by oils and creams and edible underwear."

She slipped the end of the tape in place, turned the knob until it showed in the receipt window, then closed and locked the register. "I imagine some honeymoons might be a little tense," she said, gathering up her things. "A playful approach to it probably helps. And for people who live here, it might bring a honeymoon atmosphere back into an established marriage."

He followed her out the door, then took the key from her and locked it as she reached up to set the alarm. He placed an arm across her shoulders and led her to her car. "Do you really think there's any such thing as a tense honeymoon anymore? I mean, with the virginal bride and the anxious groom?"

"There's going to be when Erica and Alex get married. Sex is something they argue about all the time. He wants it, and she's determined to do the smart and safe thing and wait until they're married."

"Good for her." He laughed softly. "But somehow I can't imagine her being tense about anything."

Chris unlocked the car, then looked around for the Viper. "Where's your car?"

"I left it at home," he said. "I've forgotten how incredible the air is here. I walked to town, visited Jacqui at Commonwealth Travel, stopped in to say hi to Brent at the fire station, then came to the shop. Incidentally, are we free Saturday night?"

For a moment Chris was surprised by the husbandly question. *Are* we *free?* She had to admit that it gave her a dangerously comfortable feeling.

"Uh . . . yes, as far as I know."

"Good. It's Dad's birthday, and Jacqui insists on having a surprise celebration at the inn."

"That'll be fun. And your father will love it." Chris let herself into the car. Paul pushed her door closed, then walked around to the passenger side. "What?" she asked. "You're not going to insist on driving?"

"Not this time." He turned toward her, then buckled his seat belt. "I want to stare at you all the way to the café."

"It's only around the corner on Bridge Street. And the Eternity scenery is much more interesting."

"It's dark. Are you getting shy with me, Christine?"

"No, I'm thinking pizza," she said, turning the key in the ignition. "And I don't want anything to distract me."

"I'll be very quiet. You know, Mr. and Mrs. Stuffed Shirt on the bench in front of the shop need some pumpkins around them and a few bundles of wheat or something."

She gave him a smiling glance as she pulled out of the parking spot. "If you're not busy tomorrow, you could pick those up at Silvas."

"Sure. But one good turn deserves another."

This time her glance was suspicious. "Really. And what did you have in mind?"

"Pumpkin pie," he said to her surprise. "That custardy one that tastes like ambrosia."

Only faintly disappointed he hadn't suggested a payment more intimate—only because she wanted to be sure the scheme was progressing, she told herself—she nodded as she turned in the direction of the café. "You're in luck. Pies are my specialty."

He reached a hand under her hair to tease the nape of her neck with a fingertip. "You seem to have a lot of specialties. Cook, baker, businesswoman, scarecrow artist. And you kiss wonderfully, too."

She laughed to distract herself from his touch. "If you're going to do something, you should do it well. Now, behave yourself, or I'll make you eat your olives."

That had intriguing possibilities. He thought about them as she pulled up in front of the café.

PAUL THOUGHT he was dreaming. But he wasn't even in bed. He was standing in the kitchen just before midnight, the utensil drawer on the floor while he smoothed the runners with a plane. Chris had mentioned that the drawer kept hanging up when she pulled on it. He'd decided to fix it now because he didn't want anything to interfere with her superior kitchen abilities—not because some part of him wanted her to have every little thing she wanted, wanted to make up to her for the terrible hurt he'd caused her, wanted her to see how much he'd learned.

And because he knew he'd never be able to sleep. All during dinner, while they'd talked and laughed over pizza, he'd been reliving that kiss in the shop. And letting his mind wander beyond it, as it used to when he'd been eighteen.

And now she was coming toward him in an almost transparent white thing that swung around her ankles as she walked. Her feet were bare, and her hair was up, wispy ends curling at her ears and her neck as though she'd just stepped out of the shower.

He could smell gardenias before she even reached him. She carried something in her hands.

"Almost finished?" she asked.

In his current mood, her presence was like a gust of wind that turned spark into flame. He turned deliberately away from her to gain control of himself.

"Almost," he replied, concentrating on the drawer. He replaced it, pulling it out, then pushing it in. It moved smoothly.

"Thank you," she said, bumping his arm with the silky thing as she reached out to try it herself. "I had no idea you were so handy. You came to Eternity with a toolbox?"

He took a step away, replacing the plane in the practical and probably antique handled carrier. "Brent lent it to me. My father wouldn't know how to replace a faucet washer, so he doesn't even own a set of tools."

Chris looked into his eyes. He felt pinned.

"I brought something to help you relax," she said, then added with a complex smile, "and to help me prove a point."

He knew this was a dangerous moment. Something could happen here that would change everything, and he was surprised to find himself ambivalent about the prospect. He wanted her with a desperation that was

becoming physically painful. But he knew that once he
made love to her, he would be bound forever. He
wondered idly, as she took hold of his wrist and pulled
him after her, if that was really why he'd left Eternity
in the first place all those years ago.

She drew him into the living room where he'd already turned out the lights, intending to go to bed
when he'd finished in the kitchen. She tugged on his
wrist until he sank to his knees on the old braided rug
in front of the fireplace. A small fire still lingered from
earlier in the evening, and she parted the screens and
poked the embers back to life. They crackled and leapt
in a low but steady flame. He felt a kinship with it. Its
twin was fanning in his gut.

"You're very intense," she said quietly, getting to
her knees beside him. She tugged up on the hem of his
sweatshirt until he took it from her and yanked it over
his head. "While I'm sure it's beneficial in some in-
stances, it can be detrimental in others. Like, at the
end of the day, when you'd like to relax and get some
sleep, and all your mind can think of is one more chore
that has to be done."

She took the sweatshirt from him, tossed it at the
chair. "T-shirt, too," she said.

He pulled it off and tossed it after the shirt. She
watched the firelight burnish his back, highlight his
muscled shoulders, gleam in his hair.

His eyes met hers, watchfully, consideringly. It occurred to her that she had to do this carefully, or she
would end up in as much trouble as she was trying to
place him.

She pointed to the floor, inviting him to stretch out.
With a last measuring glance at her, he braced his upper arms on the rug and eased his upper body onto it.

He folded his arms under his cheek and turned his face away from the fire.

"Have you ever used oils before?" she asked as she knelt at his waist and uncapped the bottle. She had to concentrate on the task. It was difficult to remain clinical about the broad shoulders tapering to a slender waist....

"All the time," he replied lazily. "Mink oil for my hiking boots and my ball glove, motor oil for the Viper, extra-virgin olive oil for—"

She cupped several drops in the palm of her hand and tipped it out in a line down his spinal column. "I meant body oils," she said, a note in her voice that was seductive, as well as scolding.

Paul felt the oil, slightly warm from her hand, trickle along his vertebrae. For a moment he thought it *was* like a special oil—snake oil, the brew hawked from wagons at the turn of the century as a curative for everything from bunions to intestinal distress. He was sure it would have about as much effect on a man's libido.

Then he began to feel the tingle. Sure his mind was playing tricks, he lay still, analyzing. There was heat running under his skin where the oil had fallen. It was subtle at first, just a mild, comforting warmth. Then Christy ran one very capable hand up the stream of oil and began to spread it across his shoulders and down his back.

He felt the heat inch up his neck. This was another form of heat, related to the gentle massage, yet fueled by that burst of flame in the pit of his stomach.

Chris's hands tingled to her elbows as she carefully distributed the oil from Paul's right shoulder to his left, then, fingers spread, down his back to his waist.

The sensitive pads of her fingers absorbed not only the oil's heat, but Paul's reaction to it.

He moved very slightly, as though simply realigning his body, but she heard the small sound in his throat and felt his muscles resist the spell of the oil.

She pressed a little harder, lengthening and gently rolling her strokes. "It's important to relax," she said, working her fingertips in spidery movements over him. "Don't tighten up. Don't resist the warmth." Her voice quieted as she shaped his shoulders with her hands, then rubbed back toward his spine and down in an easing, sweeping motion. "Everyone does that today. We keep to ourselves in our own cool little worlds, resisting warmth, afraid to open up." She stroked her way upward again, working from his spinal column out to his sides, then back in again until she reached the waistband of his jeans. "And what does it get us?"

The question had been rhetorical, but she was distracted by the firm, warm body under her hands and lingered long enough over an answer that he must have thought she'd asked the question of him.

"Safety," he replied, then added after a moment, "and loneliness."

Chris closed her ears against the vulnerability in his voice. His current position was the result of a deliberate choice on his part—one that had changed her life, as well as his. And she hadn't wanted it changed. She'd been perfectly happy with it the way it was.

Remembered pain eased the task of making things harder on him. She moved herself a couple of feet forward until she was even with his arms, then tugged one of his hands out from under his head. He didn't resist, simply closed his eyes and docilely extended the arm.

Chris massaged it from fingertips to shoulder.

When Chris moved to his other side and began to work her magic on his other arm, Paul began to feel as though he could fly. His arms were no longer weighty appendages but expertly constructed instruments of flight, destined to move his weightless body through the air like the wings of a bird or an angel, to take him higher than he'd ever been, to help him find secrets hidden from mortal man.

No, he corrected himself. The heat radiating throughout his body from that warm central core had nothing to do with esoteric discoveries, but with a very earthbound lust. And Christy was working him over with a clinically innocent detachment he was beginning to distrust.

But what he felt was so strong, so deep and urgent—and honest—that he didn't want to think it had all been called up as part of a trick.

Paul turned the arm she massaged so that he could catch her wrist. It was slender and fragile in his hand, and he rolled onto his back and yanked her over him. She fell across his chest, her eyes wide, her cheeks pink from the fire, her mouth in a startled O.

Her soft breasts flattened against his chest, nipples pearled against his own sensitized flesh.

He wasn't sure what he intended. It crossed his mind to accuse her. "You're trying to seduce me." Or to simply ask, "What do you think you're doing?"

Then he realized that he didn't care why she was doing whatever she was doing and that he had absolutely no problem with being seduced. His teenage dreams all those years ago had included a wild encounter with her in the beach grass near a fire one starry night.

This wasn't the beach, but they had a fire, and he could swear there were stars in her eyes. He wound his hand in her hair and brought her face down to his.

Chris cautioned herself to keep her head. But his mouth moved on hers with mobile skill, one of his hands cupped her head, and the other charted her with long, exploratory strokes that put her skill with the body oils to shame. Flame nipped along in the path of his fingers, down her back, over her hip, along her thigh, then back up again until it seemed her soul caught fire.

"Christy," he whispered against her open mouth. "Ah, Christy. It was supposed to be like this." He kissed her with unrestrained passion, turning them so that she was on her back and he lay over her, pinning her to the rug with his body, his tongue delving into her mouth with a greed he could no longer deny. She was his. He leaned his cheek against hers, breathing heavily. "It was always supposed to be like this."

Chris had never known such satisfaction—or such heartbreak. It *was* always supposed to be like this. But it *wasn't*. And now it couldn't be. And it was all his fault.

It frightened her to discover how closely aligned revenge was to passion and how powerful they were when used together.

She ran a hand down the wiry hair at the back of his neck, nipped his bottom lip and the line of his chin. "Yes, it was," she replied, the thickness of her voice genuine. "You and me. Forever."

His hands braced on the floor, he pushed up from her, his eyes deep and gleaming in the firelight that gilded one side of his face and put the other in shadow.

Her hands slid to his shoulders, her eyes focusing on the turbulence in his, the passion that seemed so real. *It is real,* a little voice inside her prodded. *Don't kick it back at him.*

For an instant she vacillated. But she remembered very clearly that she'd thought it had been real once before.

"I love you," he said. Then he shook his head, as though that revelation confounded him. "I . . . don't even know what that means, except that it's here." He put one fist to the middle of his chest. And it was that gesture that decided her. It implied that what he felt was stuck there, like something he couldn't swallow, or something that might choke him. "I'm sorry about our wedding."

"So am I," she said softly. "You were drunker than I realized."

He shook his head. "I mean the other wedding," he said gently. "The first one. The one where I ran and left you to face everyone alone."

She didn't say anything; she couldn't. Suddenly she had the same feeling he had—as though something was caught in her throat and about to choke her.

"Christy." He leaned closer to her, one hand stroking the hair back from her forehead, the other framing her face. "Do you love me?"

She could have said no. In the end it would have hurt him less, but this was revenge, after all. It was supposed to hurt. It just wasn't supposed to hurt *her.* And "no" would have been a lie, anyway.

"Yes," she whispered. "I love you."

With a decisive movement, he slipped both arms under her and lifted her off the rug. "I'm taking you to bed."

For a moment she couldn't find the will to resist. Then her brain assumed the task her heart refused. But she had to literally dredge up convincing resistance. "No," she said, pushing gently at his shoulders.

He stopped in the process of lifting her, her upper body in his arms, leaning against his bent knee. She saw the passion in his eyes struggle with suspicion.

"No?"

"No," she said, almost convincing herself this time. "I won't make love with you again until you *want* to be married to me."

He studied her in perplexity, then said reasonably, "But I love you. I just told you I love you, and you said you love me."

She nodded, hooking an arm around his neck to pull herself up so that she could sit back on her heels. He knelt beside her, his arm resting on his bent knee.

"You loved me the last time," she said, holding back any note of accusation. "And I loved you. It isn't loving you have a problem with. It's promising."

Frustration was uppermost in Paul's awareness, but he felt something more, a fragile grip on something he didn't understand, but didn't want to lose. He tried to hold on.

"I *want* to be married to you, Christy," he said.

She gave him a sad smile and a disbelieving look. "You want to have sex with me. That's not the same thing."

Frustration, temper, suspicion, all flared inside him and drove him to his feet. He stormed the width of the room, then back again, stopping to stand over her and point an accusing finger.

"This is another thing that hasn't changed in twelve years. In your omniscient wisdom, you think you can see inside my head and inside my heart. In reality, you're just like the rest of us. We can't read each other's minds or intentions. We can only guess and do the best we can with that. But you always think you have some magical power that allows you to read everyone like page proofs. And because you think you can read them, you think you can edit them, too. Delete this, change that, move that over here."

He reached down to catch her arm and pull her to her feet.

"You still want to make me into what *you* want me to be."

She was trembling with emotion, with unresolved passion, with the fear that he might be right.

"You think I don't know what you were doing tonight?" he demanded, giving her a little shake. "You weren't trying to help me relax. I think your intentions were quite the opposite."

"My intentions," she said, pointing to the bottle of oil with her free hand, "were to show you that you were wrong about the Honeymoon Oil."

"And why was that important?"

She lowered her gaze and heaved a ragged sigh. Both gestures were genuine. She didn't want to risk his reading the truth in her eyes. And she was suddenly very tired of this whole thing. But she was in too deep, and she knew this sudden guilt she felt would be gone in the morning. The scheme was right. It was justice. She just felt tired and defeated now.

"You forget that I do *want* to be married to you," she said. "It seemed logical to show you what you're missing by resisting our marriage."

He dropped his hands from her and turned away in exasperation. Then he turned back, both hands in his pockets.

"Then why in the hell won't you come to bed with me? Wouldn't that be a sharper reminder to me of what I'm missing?"

She looked up at him at that, shaking her head at his male obtuseness.

"I'm sure that back in Boston," she said, folding her arms, "you have women enough to warm your bed on a fall evening. What you don't have—I'm guessing, of course, since you did marry me—is a woman who will love you day or night, spring or fall, when you're being charming or when you're being a jerk. Who'll wait for you when you're away for weeks and who won't get bored with you when you're home. Someone who's always loved you, and will love you until the day she dies. What you don't have, Paul Bertrand, is me."

He was no longer thinking logically. She'd taken everything he thought he understood and twisted it until he felt as though he was caught in a giant net. But pride forced him to make one more effort to fight back.

"You're wrong about that, Christy," he said softly, cupping her head in one of his hands and looking down into her eyes. "I have you. You won't admit it, and you won't give me anything but grief, because you want to pay me back for what I did to you by torturing me." He dropped his hand and put it back in his pocket. "Okay. I've got it coming. But one day revenge is going to feel as empty to you as escape became for me. But you're not as selfish as I am. It'll be harder for you. We don't have all that long to resolve this. You'd better give it some thought. Good night."

Paul walked to his bedroom, his heart like an anvil in his chest. Christy sank to the rug and let her tears fall, unable to decide which one of them was winning—or if anybody was.

PAUL LOOKED UP from the depressing American League East standings and closed the *Courier* sports section on his dreams of the Sox winning the pennant. As far as status went, he was the only one in the world in a worse position than they were. That was saying something.

He took another slug of coffee, considered one of the onion rings he'd pushed away earlier, then decided against it. Jacqui's party for his father would take place tonight at the inn and he had to save his appetite. Christy had been cooking for him since she'd moved in as though he were some five-by-five maharaja, and her skill in the kitchen seemed to be unaffected by whether or not the two of them were getting along.

Things had been cool between them the day after their argument in front of the fire, but she'd made the most elegant chicken pot pie he'd ever tasted for dinner that night. And home-baked rolls. And blueberry cobbler from berries she'd picked near the beach.

And the menu had been every bit as delicious in the few days since. On his way out to the Peabody, he'd passed Alex Powell jogging, young calf muscles taut, T-shirt plastered to his back, sweatshirt tied around his waist. He'd felt old.

It was absurd, he knew, to feel old at thirty-one. But he'd felt old since his mother had left. And Christy's moralizing made him feel older. *I won't make love with you again until you want to be married to me.* What kind of attitude was that for a nineties woman who owned a shop that sold edible underwear?

The restaurant door burst open, and Alex walked in, pulling on his sweatshirt. He spotted Paul across the row of booths and Paul beckoned to him, resigned to spending the rest of his meal on the wrong end of an interview.

"Mr. Bertrand." Alex extended his hand, embarrassingly pleased to see him.

"Mr. Powell," Paul returned, gesturing him to sit opposite. He beckoned the waitress. "Call me Paul. I'm feeling old enough already today."

Alex looked concerned. "Something wrong?"

"All your fault. I saw you jogging and was plagued with guilt because I was on my way to have a burger and onion rings."

The waitress arrived, pencil poised over her pad. Alex grinned. "Then I guess I'm required to have a burger and onion rings to show you that your guilt was misplaced. And a cappuccino."

Paul raised an eyebrow. "Don't kids drink soda anymore?"

Alex shrugged. "I'm trying to lend a little class to my life. And I need the caffeine. Homecoming dance tonight. Erica'll want to dance all night long."

The boy didn't sound pleased at the prospect. "Is that so bad?" Paul asked.

Alex leaned back in a corner of the booth and shook his head, toying with the napkin at his place. "No. I like to be with Erica. But all she'll talk about is her dress."

"Her dress?"

"Her wedding dress. She's planning it already. She has a folder with all these pictures cut out of bride magazines, and she wants to take the sleeves of one, the skirt of another, but she wants the kind of silk like in a third one and..." He shook his head. "I forget what it is about the fourth one, but it's beginning to drive me crazy."

Paul opened his mouth to ask if they weren't a little young to be making wedding plans, then remembered that he and Christy had done the same thing at about the same time, and he'd felt quite certain about it at first. It hadn't been until it had all begun to make him feel inadequate that he'd started to panic.

It was possible that Alex was smarter than he'd been. The kid was beginning to panic *already*.

"Tell her the subject's taboo for the evening," Paul suggested. "Then talk about only what you know she'll want to hear so that she'll be too mesmerized to bring it up. How beautiful she looks, how wonderful she feels in your arms, how gracefully she dances."

Alex made a wry face. "I'm not sure I could carry that off all evening. I hate that kind of tripey stuff."

Paul raised an eyebrow again. Because he'd related to the boy's dilemma, he'd forgotten how young he was. "If you ever want to be successful in a relationship with a woman and you don't want her to talk about just what *she* wants to talk about, you have to learn to share what you're feeling. It tends to sound tripey, but they like that."

Alex took a long drink of water and polished off one of Paul's onion rings. "I wonder why you can't just get married, you know? I mean, why does there have to be all this fuss? Why does there have to be a whole town dedicated to getting people married and seeing that they stay married? And why do I have to live here?''

The waitress placed Alex's burger and rings in front of him and topped up Paul's coffee simultaneously. ''Right back with your cappuccino,'' she told Alex.

''Fate, Alex,'' Paul said, adding another shot of cream to his steaming cup. ''And you can't fight that. It's a given. You have to go from there.''

Alex glanced at him as he reached for the catsup. ''You got out.''

Uh-oh. ''You planning to do that?'' Paul asked casually.

The boy shook his head and replied candidly, ''No. Not like that.'' There was mild censure in the words that Paul was sure was unconscious. It raised the guilt he'd allowed himself to ignore since marriage had been forced on him.

Alex picked up his burger and hesitated a moment, looking out the window at the bright and beautiful afternoon. ''I do find myself wishing there was a way I could get that scholarship.''

''Maybe you will.''

Alex shook his head, apparently resigned. ''I don't think so. Like I said before, too many better candidates.''

''There's always community college.''

''But I'd still be here. And if I was here, I'd have to get married.''

Alex took a big bite of burger. Paul admired the youthful appetite that could still fit food around personal crises.

"Have you discussed this with your parents?" Paul asked. "I imagine they'd be against your taking a course of action you're not comfortable with."

Alex chewed and swallowed, then dipped an onion ring into a dollop of catsup. "They're good friends with the Silvas. They think Erica's great. *I* think Erica's great. I can't wait to—" The boy's eyes, which had lost focus as he thought about Erica, now refocused on Paul. Alex looked embarrassed and slumped in the booth. "You know what I mean."

"I do." Paul sipped his coffee and chose his words carefully. "And as wonderful as that is, it's not something on which to base decisions with results that'll last a lifetime."

"But, it's like . . ." Alex put his burger down. Paul knew this had to be important. "Like I have all these feelings for her that aren't just. . . sex. She's smart and funny and sometimes she does dumb things, but she can admit later that it was dumb. I admire that. I have a lot of trouble doing that. Sometimes she makes me feel protective, and sometimes I think she's so smart she doesn't need *me*."

Paul smiled at that; it was so familiar. It took a long time for a man to come to terms with being bested by a woman—in *any* way.

"*She* seems to think she needs you," he reminded him.

"I don't know," Alex said after a swallow of cappuccino. "Sometimes I wonder if she just needs me so she can have a wedding."

Paul remembered the dark-eyed Erica and the loving looks she cast at Alex. "I think it's more than that. And you keep forgetting that you still have eight months of school. A lot can happen in that time, things you can't even imagine now."

Alex considered that a moment and seemed to relax. He picked up his burger again. "Did you and Chris..." He riveted a questioning look on Paul as though that would define the words he couldn't form. "You know? Before you went away?"

"Make love?" Paul asked. Before a man could do it, he thought, he ought to be able to say the words. "No. We didn't."

"You didn't want to?"

Paul gave him a wry look. "Get real."

Alex laughed. "*She* didn't want to. Just like Erica. What's the point, do you think? I mean, if we're in love, what's the difference if we do it now or later?"

Paul took another sip of coffee, wishing there was brandy in it. The import of the question weighed on his shoulders. This was a nice kid. He didn't want to steer him wrong.

"Style, I think," he replied finally.

Alex blinked at him through the small round lenses of his glasses. "Style?"

Paul pushed his coffee cup aside and folded his forearms on the table. "Style. You know how important it is. Newspapers put out stylebooks for their staff so that everyone's in agreement on grammatical style."

Alex was nodding before he'd finished the thought. "But this is..." He looked around, then lowered his voice and leaned toward him. "This is *sex*. Something very personal and individual."

"Absolutely," Paul agreed. "My point is that style in general is so important that groups agree on their style when they present an image to the public. Usually it represents approaches that are tried and true create less confusion and more success.''

"But this is *love*."

"That," Paul said, pointing a finger at him, "is why it's so important to lend it some style. Love shapes your whole life. If it's good, it makes everything more enjoyable, more important, more lasting. If it isn't you can still have success and fortune, but it won't be half as exciting or rewarding as it would be if you had someone to share it.''

"So you have to love with...style?" Alex wasn' getting it. Paul tried again.

"Loving a woman with style will be the single most important thing you do for yourself in this life. Any boy in puberty can make love to a girl, but that's a natural ability, and it can feel great and mean absolutely nothing. But lovemaking that reinforces you love for one another, that touches all the deep stuff you share, that binds you together so tightly you can' imagine a future without each other—*that* has to be done with care and sincerity, with the utmost respect for one another, and with the determination tha whatever results from it is something you want to gether.''

Alex had listened carefully, and Paul had though at one point that he even understood. Then he said with a puzzled frown, "But you...don't have that Well, you do now, but you didn't for all that time you were away.''

Paul gave him a single nod. "That's why I know how critical it is.''

Chapter Seven

Louis was beaming. Paul noticed that from across the banquet table in a private dining room at the inn. His father, with Carlotta on one side and Jacqui on the other, both fussing over him, refilling his wineglass, bringing him specialties from the buffet, was lapping up his role on center stage.

"You're smiling." Chris leaned into Paul's shoulder and whispered in his ear, filling his space with some sumptuously exotic perfume. "Careful. The world becomes kind of fun when you lose that tension."

He turned to look into her eyes—and felt the impact. She had a formal glamorous look tonight, eyes subtly made up but devastatingly lethal, complexion iridescent in the low light, lips full and tinted mauve to match the rolled collar of the soft wool dress that clung to every inch of her. Her hair had been swept up with a long clip that pinned but did not contain the curly spill.

"I'm as fun-loving as the next man," he said.

"I'm glad to hear that." She toasted him with her wine. "I like that in a husband."

As she drew back into her space at the table, he leaned into her, prepared to challenge her.

"Uh-uh, you two!" Jacqui teased, mistaking his move for something sexual. "If Brent and I have to be circumspect, so do you."

Cousin Jacqui looked wonderful tonight, Paul thought. Marriage to Brent Powell certainly agreed with her. She'd lived with Louis and himself for two years as a young teen, and he'd treated her like a sister. She'd had difficulty finding happiness, and he was pleased to see that she'd succeeded at last.

"Leave them alone," Brent said. "They're more newly wedded than we are."

"And you're not all that circumspect, Jacqui," Chris said with a warning grin. "I bag your purchases from the Hideaway, remember?"

Jacqui sputtered and blushed. "Christine Bowman! I mean, Bertrand! How dare you? Isn't there such a thing as client/clerk confidentiality?"

Paul shook his head, meeting Brent's grin across the table. It was a rare treat to see Jacqui undone. "That's only for doctors and priests."

Brent turned to her. "What did you buy?"

Jacqui cooled her flushed cheeks with a wave of her linen napkin. "Never mind. You'll find out later."

Brent tried to stand and pull his wife up with him. "Well, happy birthday, Louis. Chris, we're sending the kids home with you." He ignored their howls of protest. "Good night all, it was—"

Jacqui caught his arm and pulled him back into his chair. "No, you don't. The night's still young."

Brent's sister, Bronwyn, and their great-aunts—"the ladies"—sat at the far end of the table. They leaned forward, obviously anxious to be let in on the joke.

"We can't hear," Bronwyn called. She was an attractive young woman in her thirties who presided over Weddings, Inc., taught at Pembrook College and served as justice of the peace at the Powell chapel. "What's funny? Who's still young?"

Constance, the eldest of the four sisters and the curator of the Powell museum, laughed lightly. "Not us, certainly."

"You're as young as you feel." Patience, who owned and operated a gift shop in the old gristmill Jacqui owned, was forthright and optimistic.

Violet, who always wore a shade of the color for which she was named, now sported a little cluster of the flowers pinned to her white dress. "I feel young enough to tango." She snapped her fingers as though they were castanets and winked at Louis. Then she sighed. "But my favorite partner's not up to it, I fear."

"Zamfir! Is he here?" June asked excitedly. Despite a considerable hearing impairment, she played the organ at the chapel. She turned to Violet. "I *love* the panpipes! Do you think he'd come to play at the chapel?"

Violet rolled her eyes and launched into an explanation. "Not Zamfir, June. I said 'I fear' that Louis isn't..." Tired of her task, she turned back to Paul. "To return to our original question—who is still young?"

The couples exchanged a panicked look, unwilling to repeat the conversation in front of the prim elderly ladies or Jacqui's young boys and seven-year-old girl, arranged between them. Earlier, they'd been involved in an animated conversation about ski-boarding, but now the subject at hand had their full attention.

"Not 'still young,'" Paul said, leaning toward them. "Will-iam."

"William who?"

Chris leaned around him to lend his quick thinking the support of her own. "William Powell, your father. We were talking about how young he was to run the newspaper at the turn of the century."

Patience launched immediately into one of the family's favorite stories about him and an interview he once did with Teddy Roosevelt.

Paul relaxed visibly. "Thanks," he whispered to Chris. "I couldn't put a last name to my fictitious William to save me."

She patted his shoulder. "That's all right. You did think of his first name. That was very quick, Bertrand. Still young, Will-iam. Are you used to calling women by the wrong names and having to save yourself?"

He gave her a scolding look. "No. I'm not. My private life has been far duller than you probably imagine."

"No, it's not," she denied quickly with a look of bland innocence he distrusted. "At least, not judging by ours."

"And whose fault is that?" he asked.

"Yours," she replied amiably.

Louis made a shooing gesture in their direction. "Why don't you two go find the dance floor or something? If Jacqui won't let you pitch and woo in front of her, you can do it out of sight."

"Pitch and who?" Paul asked.

Chris rolled her eyes and stood, tugging on his arm. "Come on. I'll explain it to you."

Brent grinned across the table. "Go easy on him. His mind can't connect pitching with anything but the Red Sox."

Paul allowed Chris to draw him to his feet. "I, at least," he retorted, "get to first base without help from the Honeymoon Hideaway."

Jacqui frowned at him. "Would you take your boasting to the dance floor, please? And try not to embarrass us."

"I don't dance," Paul grumbled quietly as Chris led him out of the banquet room and through the inn's entryway, crowded with half a dozen boisterous young men waiting to be seated.

At the doorway to the lounge that housed the dance floor, Chris wrapped his left arm in both of hers. "Yes, you do." Her eyes went over him gently but judiciously, paralyzing him much as a snake freezes a much larger prey with its hypnotic gaze. "We won the slow-dance competition at the senior prom, remember?"

He did not want to take her in his arms. He could still feel that Honeymoon Oil massage she'd given him days ago, and she herself was in a mood he didn't trust. She'd been verbally nipping at him all evening, glancing at him with those mistily shadowed eyes, bumping against him repeatedly, deliberately.

At first, he'd put it down to her playing the role of a wife so in love with her husband she couldn't stop teasing and touching him. But given their argument the other night, he thought she might be following her earlier tactic of showing him precisely what it was he couldn't have. That was *not* the way to win him over.

"Excuse me."

Paul turned at a tap on his shoulder. He found himself looking into the slightly bloodshot, pale blue eyes of one of the young men who'd been waiting for a table. He was elegantly dressed in a dark suit and subtle tie. But Paul suspected that the elegance wasn't even skin deep. He doubted it went deeper than the clothes.

The young man looked past him to Christy, standing just inside the lounge. "I'd like to dance with you," he said.

Before she could reply, he reached out to take her arm. Paul caught his at the wrist and pressed. Forced to let her go, the young man turned to Paul with a glare.

"She's here to dance with me," Paul said reasonably, though reasonable wasn't at all how he felt.

"Maybe she'd rather dance with me," the young man suggested scornfully, giving a yank intended to free him of Paul's grip. It didn't.

"She wouldn't."

"Can't she speak for herself?"

"I wouldn't," Chris assured him without hesitation, unconsciously moving closer to Paul.

"Hey, Brady!" one of the young man's companions called. The hail was followed by a shrill whistle. "Table's up. Come on!"

Brady turned his glare to Chris, then back to the wrist Paul still gripped. Paul freed it, and with a sneering inclination of his head, Brady walked away.

Chris expelled a suspended breath as she watched him go. "Definitely the victim of unresolved anger," she said.

Paul nodded. "Popularly known as a creep. Come on. Let's see if I remember what won us that award."

He certainly seemed to remember a lot about holding her, Chris thought as they found a spot on the small floor and turned into each other's arms. He placed one hand under her shoulder blades, the other hand catching hers and keeping it between them because of the crowded floor.

The night of their prom, she remembered, they'd danced like this and she'd felt his heart rocketing against hers. His chin had rubbed against her cheek, and they'd danced into the corner behind the band and stolen kisses.

But tonight he didn't lean down to her. He held his head erect, as though trying to keep his distance.

She reached up with the hand that held his shoulder and touched his face. She wasn't sure what prompted her—the genuine need she felt to touch him, to re-create prom night or the desire to goad him as she'd done all evening. It was becoming more and more difficult, she realized, to separate the scheme from her reality. Or was the nature of the scheme changing?

Paul thought he could get through this if she just wouldn't touch him. It was torture enough to have every curve of her body pressed against every plane of his without adding the stroke of that clever hand against his cheek.

"Please don't," he said, returning her hand to his shoulder.

"You liked that on prom night," she said in a husky whisper.

He looked down at her firmly. "I'm no longer eighteen. So don't start something you're willing to finish only on your terms."

She raised that hand again to trace the line of his jaw with her index finger. "You haven't told me *your* terms. Maybe we can compromise."

He lowered her hand again. "I have no terms. I like to live without terms. But you like them, securing all your little boundaries, tightening your private space. I don't think compromise between us is possible."

She reached both arms around his neck and leaned her head on his shoulder. "Even in the interest of . . . communicating what we feel?"

"I communicate with words," he said, holding her but still holding *himself* apart. "I've won awards for it. I told you what I felt the other night, and you told me I didn't feel that at all."

"That's because," she said softly, stroking the back of his neck, "you've never shown me. There was a part of you closed away from me all those years ago, and there still is."

She'd forgotten the scheme and in that instant had spoken with absolute sincerity and with all the frustration she'd felt as a girl when he'd held a part of himself back.

"Maybe there is," he agreed. "Do you have to know me inside out to love me?"

"No," she said. "I love you, anyway. But I have to know you inside out to understand why you can't love me."

"I do love you. I told you the other night."

"But not the way I want to be loved."

"Then why can't you accept my love the way I want to give it?"

Much as she hated to admit it, he probably had a point. And the issue didn't have to be resolved. This was only due to last another couple of weeks—if he could stand it that long—then she'd have had a part of her revenge, anyway.

She stopped dancing and tugged her arm free of his. "Excuse me," she said. "I have to stop in the ladies' room. I'll meet you back at the table."

Chris turned in a swirl of mauve wool and headed for the rest room. Once there, she slumped onto a burgundy padded stool in front of the wide mirror and groaned at her reflection. Mercifully, she was alone.

What in the hell, her reflection demanded, *ever made you think Louis's plan was a good idea?*

"Because it was very close to my plan," she replied, glancing at herself as she opened her bag and removed her compact. "And I might not have had a chance to exact revenge otherwise."

Revenge is shameful and petty.

"Tell someone who cares."

Chris patted loose powder over the shiny tip of her nose and noticed the lack of serious vindictiveness in her eyes. They were wide and blue and curiously uncertain.

"You know what you have to do," she told her reflection firmly. "And why you have to do it. He deserves it. He *hurt* you and never looked back."

He's looking back now, the blue eyes offered cautiously.

"Tough. It's too late."

Your heart isn't in this.

"My soul is."

You're going to get hurt again, her reflection warned her.

She nodded with acceptance. "But this time, so will he."

Chris breezed out of the rest room, determined to continue her campaign with renewed fervor. It didn't matter that she'd once been young and selfish and wanted too much from their relationship, that she'd thought more of her needs than of his, or that she'd been too much in charge for his easy nature. The point was she'd loved him. And he'd taken that love, tossed it off the bridge and walked away. He deserved no quarter.

"Christine."

She recognized the voice and decided to keep walking. But she was in a narrow and remote corner of the corridor between the utility closet and the telephone stall, and Brady stepped around her to block her path with a hand on each wall. There was not another soul in sight. Behind her, she could hear the sound of mixing equipment and the rattle of pots and pans in the kitchen. Ahead, the commanding voice of the maître d' called a waiter. But in this little angle of the corridor, Chris stood alone with a volatile man whose ego she'd damaged.

She tossed her head and demanded imperiously, "Yes? What is it?"

"Ooh." Brady swung one hand in a gesture of fear. "Do we have an inflated image of ourselves?"

She folded her arms, hoping it would prevent her heart from bursting out of her chest. "I don't have to inflate anything," she said, "but that's probably the only kind of woman you'd attract with your approach. Now, if you'll excuse me, Mr. Brady—"

His eyes ignited with fury and he caught her upper arm in a crushing grip. She had to concentrate not to gasp in pain.

"Don't pull that high-and-mighty act with me," he said, pushing her back against the wall. "I asked around after I saw you in the foyer, and they told me your name and what kind of shop you run. You've got to be willing to have a little fun."

Chris was now truly frightened. It was just a few yards back down the corridor to the inn's rear entrance, and she doubted anyone would hear her scream if he chose to try to take her away for the fun he described. It took all her willpower to control her fear.

"My husband is waiting at our table," she said quietly, but there was a tremor in her voice she knew he heard. She saw his eyes react to it. "You saw him. He's jealous and possessive and probably looking for me right now."

Brady leaned over her, his beer breath mingling with her fear, making her feel faint. "That's how I like you, darlin'," he said, taking her chin in his hand and forcing it still when she tried to break free. "Voice trembling, hands trembling. But I want everything else—"

Brady never finished the thought. He was yanked backward, then a big fist landed squarely in the middle of his face. He fell against the opposite wall, arms flattened against it, his eyes reeling.

"Get out of here now," Paul said, fist still doubled, arms held tensely away from his body.

Brady shook his head, focused on Paul for an instant, then flung himself at him with a bellow of rage.

Paul sidestepped him and Brady connected with the opposite wall with a sickening thunk.

Chris caught Paul's arm and tried to pull him away. "I'm all right. Please don't—"

But Brady was coming at him again and Paul shook her off, moving away from the wall.

Chris then turned her attention to the other man, catching his arm and trying to make him stop. Mindlessly angry, Brady swung on her. His level of intoxication, coupled with the disorientation caused by the blows he'd already taken, made him slightly off target. Chris ducked and his blow glanced off her shoulder.

That did it for Paul. The fury he'd done his best to contain when he'd rounded the corner and found the ham-handed creep touching Christy was now beyond his control.

He grabbed Brady by the back of his collar, turned him around and delivered the one-two combination that had won him the All Boston championship. Then he started to half drag, half carry Brady toward the lobby.

But the jerk had a head harder than concrete. He was up and struggling and threw a roundhouse Paul easily saw coming. He ducked, gave a gut punch, then eased Brady to the ground when he doubled over.

Paul looked up at the sound of women screaming and men cheering to discover he was near the maître d's podium and a group of prospective diners was pressed against the wall, apparently rethinking their decision to dine out.

At the same moment, Brady's friends appeared in a running, angry mass. Paul wasn't sure what happened next. As he went down with a large shoulder in his gut, he saw Chris fling herself, hands clawed to scratch, at one of the others. When another man reached to dislodge her, Brent joined the fray, followed by Joshua and Jason Davis, Jacqui's boys.

There was chaos, pandemonium, then the shrill blast of a police whistle. Brent was helping Paul to his feet, and Jacqui, Carlotta and the Powell ladies were clucking over Christy. Her dress was torn, and the elegant clip in her hair hung crookedly near her shoulder. Her color and her voice were high as she tried to assure everyone she was fine.

When the police left with Brady and his friends, Paul turned to Linc Mathews, the owner of the Haven Inn, to settle damages. He refused.

"Brady's a Harvard brat, comes here regularly on weekends and tries to throw his weight around because his father's some big shot in Boston. I'll get the repairs from him."

Paul looked around doubtfully. The foyer was a shambles. A mirror that had hung over an antique credenza was shattered, and a water jug and basin that had stood on it were in pieces on the floor. Several chairs in the waiting area were broken, and the bench on which he'd first seen Chris with his father that fateful night of the bachelor dinner had lost a foot and now stood at an angle. The maître d's podium was splintered.

"Why don't I cover it in the meantime," Paul suggested, "and you can pay me back if you collect from Brady."

Mathews shook his head adamantly, his impressive bearing softened by a gleeful smile. "I won't hear of it. This was as good as live entertainment."

Louis hobbled on crutches between Paul and Chris as the entourage headed for the door and the parking lot. "So do we bill you two as the Battling Bertrands and send you on the road to make our fortune?"

"Excellent idea!" Patience said. "Didn't we have an ancestor, Violet, who made a living as a pugilist, going from town to town and pitting himself against the biggest man?"

As the sisters argued over that detail, Paul stopped Chris under the spotlight outside. Her left cheek was bruised. That hurt him on two levels—first, that her beauty should be bruised was reprehensible, and second, that she should feel pain at all made him angry enough to want to set off in pursuit of Brady again.

He stroked a thumb over the bruise. "Are you all right?" he asked.

Suddenly a mass of conflicting emotions, she caught his wrist and tried to pull his hand down. He resisted, and for a moment it was a war of wills, he trying to see in her face what she was determined to hide.

She felt angry and upset without having a sure focus for it. She hated that. When she was mad, she wanted to be able to haul off at whoever was responsible.

And what a question. She hadn't been "all right" since he'd come back to town—or since he'd left in the first place.

"I'm fine," she said calmly but coolly. He freed her and she walked off in the direction of the car, pausing to embrace his father and wave a polite good-night to everyone else.

Paul stared after her in concern. Patience tucked her arm in his. "I'm sure it was frightening and upsetting for her to be accosted like that. But you know what?"

Paul leaned down to hear her as she lowered her voice.

"Sometimes, being rescued can be just as upsetting."

"I don't understand."

Patience smiled. "In my day, a woman commanded a man's respect and protection. Today, respect has to be legislated, and women are supposed to be too self-sufficient to require protection. You've put her up there on a pedestal, so to speak. You've made her special." She squeezed his arm. "She probably doesn't consider it 'cool' to admit that she likes it. But don't give up. Every woman, modern or ancient, wants to be cherished."

Twenty minutes later Paul was convinced Patience had no idea what she was talking about. He and Chris had arrived home. She'd stormed into the kitchen, glared at him when he tried to follow and ask her once again if she was all right, then began rattling things in the utility closet. Mystified, he went to the bedroom, changed into jeans and a sweatshirt—longing for his Boston College sweatshirt now being worn by a scarecrow—and went in search of a cup of coffee. Christy couldn't keep him out of his own kitchen.

He came to a dead stop in the doorway. Table and chairs had been moved aside, two-thirds of the floor had a just-scrubbed glassy sheen, and the other third was having the surface rubbed off it by a mop-wielding madwoman in crystal earrings, a striped apron over the mauve wool dress and stocking feet.

She caught sight of him, stopped and held the mop handle upright in one hand as though it were a flintlock. He wouldn't have been surprised to find it loaded.

"What?" she asked flatly.

"Coffee," he replied, folding his arms and leaning against the doorframe, "and a little civility, if you don't mind. What in the hell is wrong with you?"

As if she knew. In a very short space of time at the restaurant she'd felt great fear under Brady's threat, enormous relief when Paul appeared, delight and justification of her love for him when he'd come to her defense without hesitation, then a sudden, infuriating confusion over what it all meant.

It couldn't be that he cared that much. The other night he'd said he loved her, but she was reasonably sure that was simply because he'd wanted to take her to bed.

And it *couldn't* be that *she* cared that much. She wasn't such a fool that she'd knowingly fall into the same trap again. But even now, as they faced each other across several feet of floor tile, she found herself yearning to bridge the distance, to magically find some window in time that would take them back twelve years to that night of the prom and his proposal on the bridge.

But the thought alone was absurd. And she was so miserable she had to take it out on someone. And no one deserved it more than Paul.

"I'll tell you what's wrong!" she said, dropping the mop handle to the floor with a clatter as she tiptoed over the wet floor to the coffeepot. "I work like a dog to establish a reputation in this town as a good businesswoman and a purveyor of romance, and *you*—" she turned to point at him accusingly before yanking a mug down from the cupboard "—make it clear to everyone that I'm married to a barbarian!"

Occasionally, under the glamorous woman Christy had become, Paul caught a glimpse of the simple, organized girl she'd been, with basic values and big plans.

But at the moment she was a complete enigma. This was a Christy he'd never seen. He was both frustrated and fascinated.

"Brady," he reminded her, "had his hands all over you, and was about to drag you out the back door."

"You could have reasoned with him," she said irritably as she tiptoed carefully back, hitting dry spots and protecting the coffee with a hand cupped under it. "Or you could have taken him outside."

She tried to hand him the cup. He ignored it. "I couldn't have done either," he retorted, "because I was too angry to think. And getting him off you, not looking for a refined way to do it, was my primary concern."

"I would have thought," she said coolly, reaching for his hand, turning it palm up and placing the coffee cup in it, "that it would be impossible to dredge up that much outrage over my being manhandled when you once walked out of my life, then w-walked... back... into it...."

A horrible thing began to happen. Her eyes pooled with tears, and a sob she tried desperately not to allow refused to be swallowed. It caught in her throat, underlining every word she spoke, getting bigger and higher and bringing her closer to tears.

It had been her worst nightmare all the times she'd plotted her revenge—that she would have the opportunity, then blow it by bursting into tears and letting him see how he'd devastated her.

She didn't know where this had come from. Out of the turbulent emotions of the past half hour, but why now? She hadn't wept over him since the day after he'd left.

She tried to run past him, but he caught her arm, holding the cup away as she tried to yank free.

"Christy, listen," he said, reaching to the edge of the counter to put the cup down, but she slapped at him and he missed the Formica as he dodged her blow. The cup fell and shattered, spreading a little river of dark brown coffee on the clean floor.

But neither of them noticed. They were caught in a struggle for supremacy of the moment—she wanting desperately to escape, he wanting just as desperately to make her stay.

"Christine!" She continued to swing at him and he turned her away from him, hooking an arm around her waist and lifting her bodily off her feet. "Christy, listen!"

"Let me go!" she shrieked, madly pedaling the air. She reached behind her and tried to grab his hair.

He prevented that with his free hand and strode with her to the sofa, then dropped her onto it. She scrambled to her knees instantly, but by then he was sitting beside her, pulling her back down until she lay panting against the pillows, his hand against the back of the sofa holding her in place. Her cheeks were crimson, her eyes spitting fire.

"Paul Bertrand," she said, her voice low and breathlessly dangerous, "if you don't let me up this minute, I swear I'll hit you."

He understood finally what this was all about. He didn't move, but nodded gravely. "Go ahead. I think you need to do that."

She blinked and stared up at him, confusion warring with anger.

"I did a terrible thing to you twelve years ago," he prodded, "and you took it like a lady, a heroic lady.

Admirable as that is, I think it cost you too much. I think you're entitled to let loose, say what you feel and do what you've wanted to do ever since the moment you realized I wasn't going to show up."

He'd been braced for a hard right to the jaw, but not for the full impact of her body bolting upright and slamming into his. They ended up on the opposite end of the sofa, he on the bottom, she astride him, pounding her fists on his chest. A corner of his brain noticed that her blows were completely ineffective, but the rest of him felt the pain of her sobs as deeply as though George Foreman was the one beating on him.

Paul lay impassive under her assault, simply holding an arm out to prevent her from falling off the sofa in her enthusiasm for her task.

"You rat!" she screamed at him. "You coward, you stupid jerk, you *idiot!* Why didn't you just say you were afraid to marry me? Why didn't you just say, 'Let's wait a few months, or a year, or even forget the whole thing'? Why did you let me go to the church, believing you were going to meet me there, believing you were going to promise to love me and cherish me and stay with me forever? How could you just—?" She choked on a sob and had to stop to draw a breath. She grabbed his collar in both hands and leaned over him to whisper, "How could you just not come?"

Chris saw deep regret in his eyes as they looked steadily into hers.

"You just said it," he replied quietly. "Stupidity, idiocy, cowardice. And youth. I thought you were smarter and stronger than me, and I thought that made me inferior."

Chris remembered the intelligent, quick-witted young man he'd been, with a facility for words she'd so envied, and couldn't imagine why he'd believed that.

He gave her a sweet smile as he reached up to tuck the veil of hair behind her left ear. "I didn't understand then that there's a difference between acting as though you know everything and really knowing it."

That gently delivered criticism created opposing impulses within her. She wanted to giggle and she wanted to hit him again. She climbed off him and marched halfway across the room before turning around. When she did, he, too, was standing.

"I never claimed to know everything," she said defensively.

"I know," he agreed gently. "But when you ignored everything I said, answered all my concerns with the conviction that they were unfounded and planned our future without asking whether or not I wanted it, too, I could only conclude you must have understood something I didn't, because I didn't feel ready for that at all."

"Why didn't you tell me?"

"I tried. You never heard me."

She turned away at that, impatient with his reply.

"All right," he said, slowly crossing the room toward her. "Remember graduation?"

"Of course," she replied, her back still to him. "It was the week before the wedding that never was."

"Remember that I introduced you to a gray-haired gentleman who stopped after the ceremony to shake my hand?"

She frowned as she thought. There'd been such confusion afterward: parents, picture-taking, tearful goodbyes. "No," she answered. "I don't remember." Then she turned to him and asked carefully, "Why?"

"Because he was a writer from Boston doing research on the two world wars. He was a friend of Mr. Fox, our journalism teacher, and he'd come to offer me a summer job as his research assistant."

Chris couldn't believe she'd have forgotten something that important to both of them. Then her mind created an image of the introduction. No, it was more than an image. It was a memory. It had happened. And she'd chosen to forget it.

"The wedding," she said weakly, still trying to bring the image into focus, "was just a week away."

"And you didn't want to know anything else. As I recall, *you* told him, thank you very much but I already had a job in your father's department store."

"We couldn't have gone to Boston."

"The writer had leased a big house. He was going to put us up after the wedding. He even wanted to hire you as a typist."

Chris felt a strange disorientation as it all came back to her: the panic she'd felt at the thought of their going to Boston, at the notion that once Paul lived there, he'd never want to return to Eternity, the horror she'd felt at leaving all that was familiar to her, of abandoning their plan to one day buy the *Courier* from Mrs. Falconer and raise their children in the newsroom.

She turned to him, lips parted in surprise, eyes still focused on the past. "I was... angry at you for considering it."

He sighed, as though hearing her admit that somehow relieved him. "Yes. We fought about it. You reminded me that everything was planned, your father was expecting me to come to work when we came back from our honeymoon, and it would be selfish of us to go off and do our own thing when everyone was counting on us. I agreed, thinking there was something wrong with me because I wanted something different from The Plan.''

Chris put a hand to her forehead and walked past him, wondering when she'd blotted out that little detail. Why she'd done it was clear enough to see. When he left her at the altar, expiating herself of all guilt and simply blaming him made the pain so much easier to bear. And it made her so much more heroic, so much more the tragic figure—which, at eighteen, had had a certain dramatic appeal, despite the pain.

She sank into a corner of the sofa, admitting to herself that the abandoned bride had been a selfish little pig.

''I'm sorry,'' she said, finally focusing on him. ''Paul, I'm sorry.''

He came to sit near her, leaving a cushion's space between them. ''You've no need to be. I'm the one who did the reprehensible thing. And this whole discussion was just the long way around the point I'm trying to make. I think what upset you so much about tonight is that, although you still love me, even married me, you still have me in the role of villain. And it startled you to see that isn't the real me.'' He grimaced. ''At least, not all the time.''

She looked at him, unable to speak. *Although you still love me, even married me...* Guilt lay over her like a blanket, tightening, as though someone pulled at the ends. On the heels of what she'd just remembered about summarily dismissing his job offer with the writer, she experienced a sensation of suffocation and put a hand to her throat.

He moved closer and rubbed a hand gently between her shoulder blades. "God, do you still do that? Hyperventilate when you're shaken?" He pushed gently where he rubbed, pulling back on her shoulders. "Come on. Straighten up, make a pathway for the oxygen."

In a moment she was breathing more easily, though her conscience gasped like a stranded fish. She had to say something; she had to tell him about the scheme.

"Paul..." she began, her voice still sounding strangled.

"Just be still," he said. Then he stood and drew her gently to her feet. "It's been a long, trying evening for you. Why don't we just put you to bed and we can talk more in the morning."

"But I have to—"

"You don't have to do anything that can't wait until morning." When she resisted his efforts to draw her toward the hallway and the bedrooms, he swept her up into his arms and carried her there. He set her on her feet near the foot of her bed, untied her apron, unzipped her dress, then turned her to face him. "Breathing okay?"

She nodded, drawing a deep breath to show him, and because she needed it.

"Good. Then go to sleep and—" his brisk, cheerful bedside manner turned suddenly to a wistful sweetness "—think about what we were like in the beginning. Remember prom night, when each of us thought the other was perfect?"

That brought a reminiscent smile she couldn't have stopped had she wanted to.

"Dream about that. Who knows? Maybe we can recapture that. Good night." He kissed her on the cheek, then left the room, leaving the door ajar.

Chris sank onto the edge of the bed, staring at the opposite wall, realizing suddenly that if she told him the truth about Louis's trick, he might leave. And right now that was absolutely the last thing in the world she wanted.

Chapter Eight

There was a note taped to the inside of Chris's bedroom door. She sat up, still groggy with sleep, and tried to focus. She could see bold, black handwriting, but she couldn't read the words from the bed.

She tossed the covers aside and padded to the door. Bright sunlight streamed in through the sheers at her window, warming the floor where she stopped to read the note.

"Do NOT fix breakfast," she read. "Gone to Silvas' for *malassadas* and pineapple. Be right back. Coffee's on."

She rested her forehead against the note, last night's revelation settling like a brick in the pit of her stomach. She'd been cruelly selfish to the young Paul, and though he'd been cruel in return, he hadn't done it in retribution but out of desperation. He hadn't known what else to do.

Last night he'd matter-of-factly forgiven her for destroying that opportunity for him. That had shown her even more clearly than his physical defense of her in the restaurant had that he wasn't the villain she'd imagined him all these years.

She pushed sluggishly away from the door and headed for the shower. But what did she do now? The honorable solution would be to tell him that she was in cahoots with his father, that she'd helped Louis deceive him into thinking he'd married her, hoping to lead him to remorse for having left her and eventually to the admission that he loved her now more than ever. Then she planned to lure him to the altar and leave him there as he'd left her.

Obviously that would drive him away. So she had no intention of doing it. This was the classic case, she thought, of being destroyed by one's own ammunition.

Intent on making him admit his remorse, she'd discovered she had as much reason to regret her own behavior. And eager to make him admit love, she found herself besotted.

She stood under the spray of water, turning it as cold as she could stand it to try to jar her brain and body into action and plot her next step.

Cold, but not particularly invigorated, she pulled on jeans and a sweatshirt and went down to the kitchen in search of coffee. After the mess she'd left the night before, she'd expected to find it on the floor as well as in the pot, but Paul had apparently cleaned it up and spirited away her bucket and mop.

He pushed through the back door as she stood at the counter. In jeans and a big white sweater, he looked ruddy and cheerful, and not at all uncomfortable about their confrontation the night before.

"Good morning," he said with disarming good humor. "You get that one cup and that's it for now. Pour the rest of the pot into a thermos. We're going sailing."

"Sailing?" she repeated thinly. "Before breakfast?"

"*For* breakfast. I met Dad and Carlotta at Silvas' deli. Dad asked me if I'd take them sailing." He pulled a large, spiny pineapple out of the bag he carried, then reached into a deep drawer for a curious-looking tool. It resembled a big doughnut-cutter on a long handle.

She frowned at him and moved closer. "What is that?"

"A pineapple corer," he replied. "Don't tell me you've never seen one."

She admitted her lack of education with a shrug. "You were the one with the passion for pineapple, the guy who claimed he could survive on a deserted island in complete happiness with pineapples and *malassadas.*"

He gave her a grinning glance. "If you recall," he said, concentrating as he fitted the corer around the pineapple, "when I made that claim, I mentioned a third requirement."

The corer carefully placed, he braced one large hand around the side handles and began to turn it. The blades turned in a perfect circle, separating the meaty flesh of the pineapple from the outer skin and the core.

When he reached the bottom, he pulled up the corer, and tore away the skin to reveal the perfectly tubular edible part of the fruit.

She felt like that, Chris thought as she watched him carefully. As though she had a very large deep hole in her middle.

Paul dropped the corer, wiped his hands on a towel, then turned to give her his full attention. "Do you remember what that was?"

Until that moment, the cold shower hadn't helped her plan a course of action. Then his warm hands reached out to stroke gently up and down her arms, and she felt their warmth penetrate flesh and bone to touch the heart of her.

And she knew suddenly what she had to do. She had to keep him. Not for the time left of the phony bet, but forever. He was hers and she was his. Always had been. Always would be. She just had to help him see that.

She took a step forward into his arms. "The third requirement was me," she whispered, wrapping her arms around his waist. His arms closed around her and she leaned her cheek against his chest. Everything in her world clicked into place.

Paul drew a deep breath. Yes. It had worked. He'd known last night that the only way to draw her into his future was to force her to admit her anger about the past. Now if he could just move slowly, let her set the pace of the relationship, he might stand a chance of holding her.

What he would do if he succeeded he had no idea. All he knew at the moment was that this bright sunny morning with her in his arms was critical to his sanity, and he would deal with tomorrow tomorrow.

"You've forgotten," Chris said, tipping her head back, "that you don't *have* a sailboat."

"It seems *you*'ve forgotten," he returned, leaning down to plant a light kiss on her lips, "that I am ever resourceful. I've rented one from the Lighthouse Marina."

And that little touch was all it took. Passion sparked in her, need flamed in him, and she stood on tiptoe as he leaned down. Their lips came together hungrily, his hands moving greedily over her as she clung to his shoulders. He lifted her up, his hands cupping her bottom, and she wrapped her legs around his hips.

It was everything they'd ever felt as teenagers, trebled by absence, maturity and new discoveries. It was dearly familiar and all new—the passion of youth enhanced by time and at least a small measure of wisdom.

Chris raised her head to look at him in amazement. His slumbrous eyes met hers, dark and tantalizing. He pulled her back to him and placed his lips at the neck of her sweatshirt.

"I'd do better at this," he said hoarsely, "if you'd take that off."

She seriously considered it for a moment, then kissed the top of his head and laughed. "We're going sailing. Your father and Carlotta are expecting us."

"Call them," he suggested, his voice muffled against her flesh, "and tell them we've changed our mind. You and I are flying, instead."

She tugged mercilessly at his hair to draw his head up. "We're going sailing." She kicked at his bottom with one of the feet wrapped around him. He swatted hers with one of the hands holding her. "Or am I being bossy again?"

"You are," he replied, easing her to her feet. "But trust you to keep your head when everyone around you is losing theirs. Kipling must have known you."

She pushed firmly out of his arms. "This was all your idea, if you'll recall. Where's the thermos?"

"It was my father's idea," he corrected. "It's on the top shelf. I'll get it. You'll need a warm jacket and gloves." He looked down at her feet in their plain white tennis shoes. "And warm socks. Do you have any?"

"Of course I do. A green pair and a pink pair."

He took the *malassadas*—fat, sugared, raised doughnuts—out of the paper bag and dropped them into a quart-size plastic bag. He frowned at her while she poured coffee. "You mean those thin cotton things I put in the dryer the other day?" He rolled his eyes scornfully. "I'll lend you a pair of mine."

She returned a teasingly scornful huff. "I hope they're in better shape than your Boston College sweatshirt."

They were thick, gray wool that reached to her knees, with bright green heels and toes. "They resist water," he said, pushing one on the foot she held out from her perch on the sofa. He sat on the edge of the coffee table.

Paul smoothed the toe in place, than ran the nail of his index finger lightly down the middle of her foot. She squealed and yanked her foot back. She upbraided him with a look that held laughter at bay very precariously.

He pulled her foot back and eased the sock over her heel. "Still ticklish, still hyperventilate, still crazy about me." He grinned at her as the heel came several inches up the back of her leg. He yanked on the toe until the heel fit, then doubled it over. "Haven't grown up much, have you?" He lowered that foot and reached for the other.

"Still drink too much at bachelor parties," she retorted, "still use the juvenile technique of tickling, still crazy about *me*. What does that tell you?"

The right answer would have been that he hadn't grown up much, either. But he'd always solved his problems his way.

He leaned over to pinch her chin. "That we're made for each other."

CHRIS WAS SHOCKED and fascinated to find that Carlotta wore exactly the same kind of socks she wore. The older woman shook her head when Chris mentioned it.

"Louis forced them on me," she said. "I'm also wearing snuggies that have been out of fashion for a generation, and every sweater I own. Whose idea was this, anyway?"

"It wasn't mine," Chris assured her. "I can't swim, so I prefer to enjoy the ocean from land or a nice sturdy pier. But Paul's always loved the water."

Carlotta nodded knowingly. They sat together in the sunny stern of the boat. But Chris noted that though they weren't even out of the harbor, the wind was strong and cold, and she was already grateful for the socks.

"Got that from his father. He and my husband used to fish together. I've been sailing a time or two, but I've never been that comfortable with it. I usually limit my immersions in water to baptism, bathtime and old-lady exercise routines at the pool where you can hold on to the side."

Chris giggled and passed Carlotta a doughnut. "A woman after my own heart."

"HOW ARE YOU TWO getting along?"

Paul turned to his father at the question. He had

propped him up on his crutches at the helm, and he was guiding their path across the harbor.

"Like most husbands and wives," Paul replied, somehow feeling it was important that his father think he had his life under control, primarily, he guessed, because Louis had never managed that with his. "Some days very well, some days not."

"So..." Paul heard a careful pause in Louis's voice. "You're staying with it?"

Paul answered honestly. "For the moment. Tomorrow writes itself."

Louis didn't like the sound of that. "You mean there's a chance you'll leave her again?" he asked, knowing that subtlety got him nowhere with Paul.

"I mean," Paul replied impatiently, "that tomorrow's a mystery. You understand that. Only with you the mystery wasn't the next day, but the next woman."

Louis absorbed the blow of Paul's accusation like a losing fighter just trying to stay on his feet, to last out the round. The boy was right in a way: he just had a poor grasp of the circumstances.

Then, to Louis's complete surprise, Paul dropped his hostile stance.

"I'm sorry," he said with what might have appeared to someone else as a lack of conviction. But Louis knew his son. For him to have formed the words at all, he had to have meant them. "I don't mean to react that way to you. I don't even ... want to. It just happens."

Those were the most encouraging words Louis had heard out of his son's mouth since he'd arrived. But he knew revealing that was not a good idea.

He nodded as he studied the horizon, his expression carefully neutral. "I understand. It's a habit of long standing. And I don't mean to pry. I'm just...interested." He knew better than to say he cared.

Paul spread his arms in a gesture Louis read as meaning he understood and accepted his explanation. "Let's just let each other...live our lives. Without interference."

"Of course," Louis replied amenably, lying through his teeth.

As the sun rose higher, the wind settled to a steady blow. The rented sailboat tacked across the harbor mouth as they ate Portuguese pastry and pineapple and drank coffee from mugs Chris had remembered at the last moment.

As Louis and Carlotta admired the spectacular view of the small town in the curve of the harbor tucked safely behind a hurricane wall, Chris went to join Paul at the helm.

He saluted her with his mug. "Glad you remembered these," he said. "I'd have hated to have been fourth in line to use the thermos lid. I'd have expired of the cold before my turn."

It was comfortable to lean into him and smile. "Sometimes there's an advantage to having a bossy, organized woman aboard." She pressed mercilessly. "There's an important philosophical message here."

His arm came around her, the mug still in his hand, and he laughed. "I got it," he said. "On the picnic of life, someone has to remember the mugs."

She wrapped her arm around his waist and enjoyed being pinned to him as he brought the mug to his lips. He sipped his coffee, then looked down at her, caught in the crook of his arm, and smiled. The gesture was both warm and dangerous. And she thought with wry acceptance how that defined him—if parameters that broad could be considered definition. That was what had always worried her. What worried her now.

Paul saw that in her eyes. Deep happiness curiously mingled with some mysterious concern.

"What are you thinking?" he asked, unconsciously tightening his grip on her.

She kissed his chin and admitted candidly, "That I love you more and understand you less than I did when we were kids. I wonder why that is."

He kissed her forehead and looked out at the bright blue horizon beyond the hurricane wall. "Because you trust me more, I guess." Then he frowned. "Though, why *that* is, I can't imagine."

"Could it be," she suggested quietly, "that I've finally, truly, forgiven you?"

Paul looked into her eyes and saw love there. Not the adoration of the young Christy, or the bridal blush she'd worn the morning she'd explained that he'd married her. This was love. Real love. She knew him and she loved him, anyway. He'd hurt her and she loved him, anyway. He was deeply affected by that knowledge.

But before he could act on it, there was a loud shriek from the stern. Carlotta leaned over the side of the boat, both hands stretched out toward the water.

Paul's first thought was to turn to his father and ask him what was wrong. But he wasn't there. He wasn't there!

"Louis!" Carlotta screamed. Paul cleared the few steps that separated him from Carlotta.

She turned to him, her face white, her lips trembling. "He stood because his leg was cramping and he . . . he just lost his balance!"

"All right," Paul said calmly. "He's wearing a life jacket." And as he said the words, he scanned the water as the wind whipped them across the bay. He blinked, certain he had to be missing the figure bobbing in the bright orange.

"No!" Carlotta said, her voice high and urgent as she pointed to the jacket propped against the storage chest. "He was taking if off to put his jacket on! That's when he fell."

Paul's journalistic mind was analyzing the situation even as he put one foot on the chest, the other on the rail and leapt over the side. He wasn't doing this because he loved Louis and was afraid to lose him. He was doing this because any fit young man with any humanity would jump in after an old man whose leg was in a cast.

The water was shockingly cold, like being locked in a freezer. Paul shot to the surface just in time to see his father's gray head bob out of the water a remarkably long distance away, a hand raised high. He heard the women shouting. He started for Louis with long, even strokes.

Chris, heart pounding, saw Paul swim competently, if a little awkwardly in the jacket, toward his father. His strong arms ate up the water, and she felt a measure of relief—until she realized how the sturdy sailboat also ate up the water—in the other direction! She had to turn the boat!

She ran to the wheel and gave it a hard twist. A corner of her mind heard Carlotta shout, "No!" but she was too intent on her purpose to absorb the warning in her tone.

The boat bucked crazily as sails flapped and fought the wind. Carlotta grabbed the rail. Chris, not knowing what to do, freed the wheel and sank to the deck as the boat swung in a wild circle. Then the wind found it and sent it sailing ahead.

Chris pulled herself to her feet as Carlotta stumbled toward her.

"Do you know what to do with the sail to turn?" she demanded.

Carlotta shook her head. "We'll have to take it down! But I've never done it."

Chris visually followed the line from the sail to the cleat near the railing. They tugged at it together until they'd pulled it free. It ran out of their hands and the boat's rapid progress slowed immediately, though it didn't stop.

"We have to tie the line down!" Carlotta directed. The boom fought them until Chris took up the slack in the line, then secured it to the cleat again with a pathetically ordinary knot she prayed would hold.

The sail was finally held to the boom by Carlotta's body as she fought to tie it down. Chris ran to the controls and turned the key to start the engine.

"IF YOU'D TOLD ME you wanted to go swimming," Paul said, fitting his jacket onto his father, who was bobbing beside him with an arm on his shoulder and looking robust considering the circumstances, "I wouldn't have bothered renting a boat."

Louis watched Paul's face as he secured the ties at the front of the jacket. He'd expected anger and criticism. He was surprised to find him with a sense of humor. Maybe Chris was making more headway than he'd thought. And maybe he, Louis, was making just a little.

"Forgive an old man's loss of equilibrium," he said.

Paul grinned at him. "Sure," he said.

Louis safely in the jacket, Paul turned to look for the boat, knowing it could have covered a considerable distance in the time it had taken him to reach his father. He sobered at the new dilemma. Two women with no knowledge of sailboats were alone on one with a strong wind blowing toward the mouth of the harbor and the open sea. Two women who didn't swim.

Paul swore roundly under his breath, examining his options. The only one feasible seemed to be to swim the considerable distance to shore, then dispatch a Coast Guard boat for the women.

"Leave me here," Louis said, physically pushing him in the direction of shore. "I'll be all right in the life jacket. You've got to get help for Chris and Carlie, and you'll swim faster alone."

"They're all right for the moment," Paul said, grabbing a fistful of his father's jacket. "Come on. We're—" He stopped when he saw the boat jerk wildly in the distance, then turn in a drunken circle. "What are they doing?" he demanded of no one in particular.

"Oh, God," Louis said, his voice thick with concern. "They're trying to turn. With the sail set!"

"Take the sail down!" Paul shouted futilely across the waves. Then, as though he'd been heard, he saw the sail slacken and fall.

In a moment, they heard the roar of the engine.

Louis said incredulously, "They did it! They're turning around to come for us!"

Paul watched in amazement as the boat completed its turn and headed for them in a straight line. Christy was full of surprises.

"Well. There," he said, keeping a tight grip on his father. "Now, if they don't run us down, we're home free."

Chapter Nine

"I do *not* have to go with you," Louis told the emergency medical technicians who met the boat at the marina in response to Paul's radio message. "In fact, I'll see that you're both handsomely compensated if you'll take me to the Haven Inn for happy hour."

"Got to make sure that leg's still okay," one of the young men said as he and his partner lifted the stretcher into the back of the ambulance. "And you've been in very cold water longer than is healthy for a man of your age."

"In Scandinavia," Louis said defensively, "they jump into cold water deliberately!"

"This is New England, sir," the other technician said with a seriousness that made Louis's companions look at each other in amusement.

"Carlie? Paul?" Louis shouted, now out of sight. "Isn't anyone coming with me?"

"I'll go," Carlotta volunteered. "He's less likely to fuss at me."

"We'll be right behind you." Paul caught Chris's hand and headed for the car.

"You have to change out of those wet things," Chris insisted. "We'll stop at the house. It'll only take a minute. Here." She pushed the thermos into his hands and shoved him out of the way as she got behind the wheel, relegating him to the passenger seat. "You drink and warm up while I drive."

"You're getting bossy again," he said as she pulled out of the driveway. His tone was noticeably free of criticism, despite the words.

She glanced away from the road to grin at him. "I drove a sailboat across the mouth of the harbor to save two drowning men," she said airily. "I feel invincible."

And she did, too. He could see it in the sparkle in her eyes and the color in her cheeks. He adored her for it, but couldn't resist the urge to tease.

"I hate to burst your bubble," he said. "But neither one of us was drowning. *I* saved the man who might have drowned."

"Of course," she said. "I imagined you'd have walked your father back to shore on the water."

"I'm not saying you didn't make an important contribution," he conceded, pouring the last cup of coffee. He needed it more than he was willing to let her see. "But I did the serious lifesaving stuff. All you did was pick us up."

"Who wrapped you in blankets? Who found your father's brandy stash and poured it down you?"

He would never forget how surprised and pleased he'd been that she'd figured out how to get back to them. He knew many women who were brilliant in complicated business deals or could intelligently discuss psychology or the economy, but who were useless when it came to common sense.

But Chris was as grounded as a daisy. He'd always loved that about her. Now he loved it even more. He'd have never left his father to go for help, and he wasn't sure the old man would have made it all the way back to shore in that cold water.

"Actually," he said, reaching a hand along the back of the seat to trace the rim of her ear with his forefinger, "I think you were wonderful. You saved the day for all of us."

She gave him a quick modest glance. "I guess Carlotta had a little something to do with it. She's the one who knew the sail had to come down. I'd have fought it all day, trying to figure out what to do."

"We'll get you some sailing lessons."

She sighed. "Well, with any luck, I'll never be in a sailboat again."

"You will," he assured her, his fingertip moving down to her jaw, then down her throat to the collar of her coat.

She gave him another glance, this one startled and hopeful. He was happy to see that.

"I will?"

"I have a sailboat in Boston," he explained. "When you come back with me, I'll teach you how to sail."

"Come back with you?" she breathed, glancing in the rearview mirror and slowing down. She was no longer giving the operation of the car her full attention.

"Yes," he said. "But we'd better talk about it later, when I'm sure my father's all right and we're back home again. Want me to drive? You look pale."

"DIDN'T I TELL YOU I was fine?" Louis demanded when they were all on their way home again several hours later. He'd received a clean bill of health. "Not only that, but my leg's healing nicely."

"But you did need a new cast," Carlotta said.

"Even my blood pressure was normal after all that."

"That's because you spent all that time venting at *us*. You don't keep anything to yourself. Your kind of man makes other people's blood pressure rise."

Paul helped Louis into the chair he occupied in Carlotta's den while Carlotta took Chris into the kitchen to share some culinary delight she insisted they take home.

"Where's your remote?" Paul asked, glancing around him.

"Never mind that." Louis put a hand on his son's wrist and pointed to the ottoman. "Sit down a minute. I want to talk to you."

Paul looked at his watch. "Dad, I'm beat and you need your rest. I'm—"

Louis's gaze never wavered. "Please."

Reluctantly Paul sat.

"Thank you," Louis said seriously, "for jumping in to save me. That cast was dragging me down."

Paul nodded. "Sure. All's well that ends well."

"The thing here," Louis said, leaning toward him, "is that it won't be over between you and me until the day I die, then it'll be too late for us to end well. And I want that before I die. I want you to have understood me. I want you to know that..." Louis paused, his voice suddenly husky. "That no matter what happened between your mother and me, I always—always—loved you. And I do now. And I would have if you'd thrown me an anchor, instead of jumping in to save me."

Paul hated to keep hitting this wall that came between them, particularly since, on the surface at least, they seemed able to find more ways around it lately. But when it came down to basics, to his childhood and his mother, he couldn't see how they would ever come together on it.

But for the first time, he wondered if they could find a way to save what they had.

"Dad," he said gently, "I know you loved me. I know you still love me. And I guess I'm finding that I love you in a way I can't control. Blood calls to blood, I guess. I don't know. I know I care about you. But I don't think we can ever have the closeness you want.

"I loved my mother," Paul went on, his own voice tightening and growing quiet. "You hurt her, and what you did sent her out of my life. I . . . can't forget that. I can't forget how it made me feel, how it rattled my whole life and made it different."

Paul looked into the misery in his father's eyes and wanted desperately to erase it. The thought confounded him. He even wondered for a moment what had changed that in him.

He put a hand on his father's on the arm of the chair and squeezed. "I don't want to be your enemy for the rest of our lives. But I think that's something we just can't settle. So can we just . . . go around it and find whatever else it is we can share?"

Pain seemed to be trying to pull Louis down like the waters of Eternity Harbor had tried to do that afternoon. And Paul couldn't pull him up from this, because he didn't know. And Louis had resolved years ago that he'd never be the one to tell him. So he raised his own chin out of the water and decided that if this . . . this half a relationship was all he could ever have with Paul, he would settle for it.

But, by God, he would see that Paul had something better to fill his life than Laurette had given him. He'd done well with Christy. His little plot had been a good move.

He placed his other hand over Paul's. "Yes," he said. "I think we can. Thank you. Now, you take that wife of yours home and praise and reward her for her quick thinking."

Paul stood. "I intend to."

"Aha!" Chris said from the doorway. She turned to Carlotta, standing beside her. "You heard that, Carlie. He said he would reward me. I have witnesses, Paul."

"If he gives you stocks or negotiable bonds," Carlotta said in a stage whisper, "remind him that I threw them the life ring."

"You hit me in the head with it," Louis said.

They all laughed at the memory as Carlotta saw them to the door, then waved them off.

THEY HAD SO MUCH to talk about. Everything was changing. They should discuss where they stood, what they intended—what Paul had meant when he'd told her he would teach her to sail when he took her to Boston.

But the moment Paul pushed open the front door, words seemed not only unnecessary but irrelevant. Chris was walking beside the man she loved into the house they shared, and into the dream that had haunted her since he'd become a part of her life all those years ago.

For all intents and purposes, she was Mrs. Paul Bertrand. Everyone in town believed she was. Her parents believed she was. And so did Paul.

In Chris's heart, she'd been Mrs. Paul Bertrand since prom night, 1982.

Paul closed the door behind them, then froze where he stood as Christy turned to him. She was reading his mind. Or her eyes were reflecting what she saw in his, because her soft gaze was filled with longing and passion and the love that seemed to have blossomed and burgeoned with the mature and fulsome Christy.

He took a step toward her as she stretched out a hand to him. He caught it with his and drew her the rest of the way into his arms. They clung together for a mystified moment, the feelings too big, the reality too strong for action or words.

Chris clutched at his sweater, and he wound his fingers in her hair. They held each other as the power ran between them, fed by twelve long years apart.

Finally he tugged her head back and looked into her eyes. "I love you, Christy," he said softly. "I love you more than anything. And I need you."

"Oh, Paul." The words ran over her like perfumed oil. They were everything she'd ever hoped to hear. "I love you, too. Please need me as much as I need you."

He kissed her slowly, deliberately. Then he kissed her again. "I *want* to be married to you, Christy. I swear to God, I do."

Her smile was brilliant, her heart full—for in that moment she truly forgot that he wasn't.

He took her hand and led the way to his bedroom.

It was dark and cool and smelled of the clove-and-orange pomander she'd placed in his closet.

She'd dreamed of this a hundred thousand times. The way his hands slipped under her sweater and pulled it over her head. The way he unclasped her bra and let her bead-tipped breasts spill free.

She'd marveled over the mental picture, imagined the whispered words they'd exchange. But she'd never been able to guess how it would feel.

And she found the reality almost more than her senses could bear. Every cell seemed to acquire a life of its own, every nerve ending to tremble like the leaves of an aspen in the breeze.

When he cupped the back of her head in one hand and tipped her backward onto the bed, she felt transported, as though this were happening to her in some far-flung region of the universe. This was something she'd never known.

He placed a knee between hers on the bed and leaned over her to put his lips to her right breast. He kissed and nipped, then caressed it with his hand as he moved his mouth to the other. She felt as though she'd been infused with life in its purest form.

She caught a fistful of his sweater, intent on pulling it off, but the coordination required to accomplish such an action was destroyed by a line of kisses down the middle of her body, then the feel of his lips at the waistband of her jeans.

He pushed up onto his knee, unfastened the button and drew down the zipper.

She guessed she was as near to ecstasy as it was possible to be, and there was still so much more to—

Thought fled as she felt his fingertips invade the waistband of the jeans, the lacy elastic of her panties, and begin to tug them down. Sensation bubbled the length of her, following the path of the fabric over her hips, along her thighs, down her legs. Off.

She was as responsive and eager as Paul had imagined she would be when he'd been a dreamy youth. He'd often imagined her clinging to him, whispering endearments in his ear, waiting for him to make her his. But he'd never suspected that she would feel like this. That she'd be like pulsing silk in his hands, that he would feel her love for him as his fingertips traced her body, that she would make him forget the pleasure in store for him and think only of what he wanted to give her.

He whispered her name as he lay beside her and gathered her in his arms.

Chris was awash with sensation. His kisses touched her face, her throat, her breasts, her belly. And all the while his hand stroked her hips, her thighs, outside, inside, dangerously close to that part of her suddenly ticking with a need growing more and more desperate.

She hitched a knee over him, whispering his name. He caught it, pulled it a little higher over him and dipped a fingertip inside her.

No knowledge—imagined or real—could have prepared her for how that felt, for how her body would react. It began to riot, to fill her with feelings she'd never suspected it capable of. It warmed and fluttered and sped toward something she'd read about and heard discussed, but never experienced.

And then it struck her like the swish of a comet's tail. Heat, dazzle, power, the DNA of a star. She uttered a gasp of surprise as her body shook with it, filling her with indescribable pleasure, receding, then filling her again, until it drew away slowly one final time, leaving her stunned and still.

A mysterious note intruded upon the pleasure Paul took in *her* pleasure. There was something . . . out of place here. Something he should think about, take a moment to consider.

But she placed a small hand under his sweater, then found her way between his T-shirt and his flesh, and the thought fled.

"Paul!" Chris's whisper was urgent. As urgent as the hands that pushed his sweater and T-shirt up, impatient to remove them. He caught the fabrics and pulled them over his head.

Her body still pulsed with pleasure, and she was eager to share it with him, to take him where she'd been. She knelt beside him and traced a line of kisses across his shoulder, then down his muscled chest and over his ribs to the hollow at his waist.

He'd changed into cotton slacks before going to the hospital, and she unbuttoned and unzipped them. She did as he'd done, and drew slacks and briefs down together.

She studied him in the darkness, his flesh glowing like gold, his body as ready for her as she was to receive him.

Paul reached for her to pull her down beside him and simply hold her, wanting to stretch the moment, stretch his tolerance for the agony of going slowly, stretch the universe to encompass all he felt.

But her hands were moving over him, she dipped the tip of her tongue into his ear and reached down to explore him with her fingertips, and he could take no more.

He tucked her under him and shifted to enter her. He went slowly, withdrew, then thrust deeper—and, in confounding surprise, felt the barrier of virginity. But she held him tightly, lifted up against him, whispered his name with a sound that dubbed his own desperation for her.

"Love me," she insisted, wriggling against him. "Love me, Paul."

He pushed through the barrier, absorbed her little cry of pain with a pain of his own, then forgot everything but the eager way she moved against him, the rightness with which they moved in concert, the pleasure that rose between them like a piece of music he'd never heard before.

Chris was aware of discomfort for only a moment, then she was conscious of nothing else but having her lifelong dream fulfilled—of being one with Paul.

Arms holding each other fast, body to body, legs entwined, they rode the moment together like some new and single entity.

Paul felt the power of his release deep in a part of him he'd forgotten was there—some youthful corner where idealism and perfection had been put away, awaiting friendlier times. And as he filled Chris, he felt his own body fill with hope and promise.

As pleasure rocked Chris a second time, she trembled under its impact, feeling her own life tremble around her. Being filled with Paul was like being connected to a power source that lit every little corner of her being, charged every moving part of her body.

Dusk had turned to darkness when Paul finally moved beside her and pulled her into his arms. They lay together in silence, shaken by the lovemaking for which they'd waited so long.

Reality dawned slowly. Paul surfaced from his haze of wonderful well-being and remembered the barrier that had slowed his entry. He remembered feeling fascinated and flattered and confused. Virginity was a curious condition for a woman who'd claimed he'd been "divine" on their wedding night. He propped himself up on an elbow to look down at her.

Her eyes still closed, Chris slipped off his shoulder to the pillow, cocooned in their cozy aftermath. She protested with a little groan, wondering at the intrusion. Then it hit her like a sledge. Virginity! That was a little detail she'd blotted from her consciousness when Paul had said with such sincerity that he *wanted* to be married to her.

She remembered only that she wanted to be married to him—to make love with him. She'd somehow forgotten that he'd notice when he made love to her that no man had ever done so—himself included.

She opened her eyes, prepared to have to come clean and tell him everything. The prospect was both horrifying and tempting.

But he was smiling, his dark hair tumbled over his forehead, his eyes filled with amusement and a curious compassion. She looked up at him, lips parted in wary disquiet.

"I presume this means," he said softly, "that I was not as divine on our wedding night as you led me to believe."

Surprised by his interpretation of that moment, she was at a loss for words. Then his eyes grew serious as he asked in disbelief, "You've *never* ... made love?"

That was easy to answer. She felt herself relax as she smiled at him. "You were in Boston," she said. "I was here."

Paul felt his heart stop. Air left his lungs, and every function of his body subsisted for a full moment on the words Chris had spoken. He couldn't speak or even think. He could only feel. Love.

"Oh, Christy," he whispered as his heart began to pump again. "Christy." He opened his mouth over hers and drew her slowly, carefully, inexorably back to passion. Emotion rolled over and over him as they clung together in the middle of the bed, helpless but happy victims of their desperation for one another.

She promised him love eternal, and he swore he would always be there to accept and return it. It was midnight when they finally drew apart.

Chris left the bed and returned with sandwiches and cocoa. They sat up against the pillows, his free arm around her, their legs entangled, as they ate and talked.

"I guess buying the *Courier* now is out," Chris said, "since you're an important fixture at the *Globe,* but it might be a fun thing to do when you get tired of traveling."

"Possibly," Paul said, taking a bite of a dill pickle, then handing her the remainder. "You have no problem with moving to Boston?"

"No," she replied honestly. "I can get someone to run this shop full-time and open another one there. I imagine Boston would have use for a shop like Honeymoon Hideaway." She frowned at the pickle, then at him. "Or would I be banned in Boston?"

He shrugged. "Some areas, maybe. Otherwise, it's as lively as any other town, despite its reputation. When do you want to go?"

When? Chris tried not to betray concern as she chewed on the pickle. When? When they were *really* married, that was when. Though how she could accomplish that without explaining, and how she could explain without completely alienating him, she wasn't sure. She had to think.

"You still have a couple of weeks' vacation, don't you?" she asked.

He nodded, reaching to the bedside table for the cocoa. "Yeah, but Dad's in pretty good shape now, and Carlotta's happy to keep him there until he's comfortable without the crutches. There's not much need for me to stay."

"You're forgetting the bet," she said, fighting the little clamp of fear that was beginning to supersede her joy. This was getting entirely too complicated. And she'd been crazy to block out all the problems in the interest of making love with Paul without first explaining.

He grinned at her and she quickly changed her mind. No, she hadn't been crazy. She'd have done anything to hold him to her long enough to prove to him how good they could be together, how right it was for them to be married.

"It wouldn't affect the bet," he said, kissing her temple. "We'd be together—we just wouldn't be here. But you're probably right. You'll need time to decide what to do about the shop, and I need time to . . . get reacquainted with my life. I've spent so much time lately analyzing the world that I haven't given much thought to what I want."

"And what's that?" she asked, feeling the relief of an undeserved reprieve.

He took the half-eaten sandwich from her hand, dropped it on the tray on their knees, then put the whole thing on the floor. He pulled the blankets up over their heads and pulled her down with him into the bed. She began to giggle helplessly.

"You," he said, planting a kiss on her breast. "You."

"YOU'RE AWARE, I suppose," Paul asked as they walked leisurely down the road toward Honeymoon Hideaway, Chris's arm tucked in his, "that at the office I'm known as the Brain of Back Bay?"

Chris, the hood of her royal blue coat thrown back, smiled up at him. She was a mass of contradictions this morning, caught between absurd happiness and crushing guilt, sometimes experiencing both emotions within the space of five minutes.

But at that moment she was so happy she could have burst. The sky was bright blue, the morning crisp and cold, and the maples and oaks lining the road bleeding red and gold. And Paul had love in his eyes. Not simple lust, not the old affection, not just passion—but love. Real love. She could have died at that moment and not regretted a thing. Except that she felt far too alive to expire.

"No, I didn't know that," she said, putting her cheek to the upper arm of his leather jacket as they continued to walk. "Brent said the rumor is they call you the *Bane*...."

He slanted her a scolding look. "No. He's obviously misunderstood. And I only mention my title because I'm about to live up to it. I had the most brilliant idea during the night."

"I know," she said. "I was there."

"Not that idea. Although it was a fine one. All four times. I mean the one that came to me when you were asleep on my shoulder and I was staring at the ceiling."

They stopped and checked the traffic before crossing School Street. Chris's gaze wandered to the square of rich green grass and the minuteman monument. "What was that?" she asked.

"I think we should get married again."

Chris stopped in the middle of the sidewalk to stare up at him. Behind her she could hear children calling to one another and laughing as they raced to school. Around them, light morning traffic hurried to and from Eternity as local merchants went to work and others headed to industrial jobs out of town.

"Get married again?" she repeated dumbly.

He seemed surprised by her surprise. "Yeah," he said. "To prove to ourselves and everyone else that it's real."

"But..." She didn't know why she wanted to protest. This was what she'd wanted all along. And now, even though her motivation had changed, a real wedding would give her validity as Mrs. Paul Bertrand. She'd have it all. Except a clear conscience. And a marriage license. Panic dried her throat.

Paul, obviously mistaking her reticence for a need to be convinced, took her shoulders in his hands and laughed with deep and genuine good humor. "What did you wear to the other one?"

"What did I—?"

"Wear," he finished for her. "When we got married at the chapel, what were you wearing?"

"Ah... pants and a sweater, I think."

"Well, see? There." He raised both arms in a gesture of displeasure. "You should have been in white with a long veil and half a dozen attendants." He took her by the shoulders again and shook her gently, his smile still in place. "And I want to remember it, Christy. I want to hear you promise to love me, and I want to look into your eyes when I promise you. I want it to be everything we thought it would be all those years ago. What do you say?"

She said nothing. She couldn't. His enthusiasm for a second wedding when there hadn't been a first just rubbed salt into the wound of her guilt, and compounded her panic. She wondered if her godfather, the judge, *would* really help.

He pulled her along as he continued to walk. "And I think we should go somewhere really special. I know this little villa in Mexico where I'm treated like royalty."

"Paul—"

"We can take a leisurely cruise. We'll still save the Bahamas for our fifth anniversary."

"But you—"

"Or we can fly to save time. They have..." And he talked until lunchtime. He unpacked an entire shipment of Christmas freight for her, then ran to the deli for sandwiches.

She found a curious thing happening to her. It was as though she'd turned her conscience off and allowed her demanding self full reign. She began to wonder what the harm would be in simply following through with his plan. Each of them would get what they wanted. Paul wanted her, and she wanted him— legally, morally, really. This way, she could have him, and he would never suspect that the wedding for which he felt such remorse had never taken place.

Wasn't Dear Abby always advising spouses not to reveal their indiscretions? Assuring them that it might assuage guilt, but would also hurt the other party and wedge a rift between them that nothing would ever repair?

"Paul," she began. "What... what if we did it *all* over again? The blood tests, the license, threw in a little china pattern shopping...?"

He kissed her soundly. "I like the way you think."

This was a solution tailor-made to finally bring her and Paul together in the way God had always intended. She should take advantage of it.

A cloud passed over the sun as she held that thought, darkening the sidewalk beyond her window, darkening the shop. She went to the window and winced up at the pewter sky, suspecting this was a plan in which she should not have presumed to involve God.

Chapter Ten

Chris poured two cups of coffee and placed them beside the cinnamon crullers, then carried her tray to a small table in the corner of Silvas' deli where Louis was poring over the *Courier*'s sports section.

He folded it and put it aside the moment she placed the tray on the table. "Thank you, Chris. I've grown so accustomed to being waited on," he said, helping her unload the tray, "that I don't know how I'll adjust when I'm completely healed."

She put the tray on the empty table behind them. The deli was over its early-morning breakfast rush and had settled into a quiet pace, a few patrons lingering over coffee and morning papers.

Chris smiled across the table at Louis. They'd met like this every few months in the years since Paul had left, but they'd never discussed him. They'd simply kept in touch with each other, caught up on personal news. But today she wanted to talk about Paul.

She emptied the contents of the tiny plastic cup of cream into her coffee and stared into it as she stirred.

"Louis..." she began hesitantly. Then she looked up at him, eyes wide and concerned. "I have a problem."

He smiled with understanding rather than surprise. And the smile reminded her achingly of his son.

"I know." He took a pillbox from his pocket, selected a small white tablet and took it with the water she'd also brought. He drank the water, then set the cup between them with a little thump. "I believe we have the same problem. Paul."

She took a sip of coffee, then put the cup down and leaned back against the slats of her folding chair. "He just asked me to marry him, Louis," she said gravely.

He frowned. "But he believes you're already married, doesn't he?"

"He does. He wants to do this so that I can have the white wedding I'd always dreamed about as a girl and so that he can..." She had to swallow a lump in her throat. "So that he can remember it this time. He wants to hear us promise each other that we'll be in love forever."

Louis grinned broadly and reached across the table to cover her hand with his. "Chris! This is success! You almost have what you want."

Then he looked into her face and saw that she wasn't viewing this in the same way he saw it. He tightened his grip on her hand. "What is it?"

She leaned an elbow on the table and put a hand to her head. It was pounding—had been pounding since Paul's announcement yesterday afternoon.

"I can't do this anymore, Louis. I know I promised, and I did the best I could...but now everything's changed. I love him, Louis. I have to tell him."

"No," Louis said sharply, firmly. He knew his son. He could not—*would* not—let her do this.

When she looked up at him in hurt surprise, he lowered his voice and gave the hand he held a little shake. "No," he said more gently. "He won't understand, at least, not yet. He needs more time with you to know how deeply rooted his love for you is."

"But, Louis, he's different," she explained urgently. "He's not what we thought. Oh, I don't know if we misunderstood or if he's truly changed, but he's different! I can't go on letting him think—"

"You can," Louis insisted quietly, trying to will her cooperation. This was what he'd wanted all along— what his plot was intended to bring about. "You must. He's riding on a high of discovery right now. He's home, we've repaired a few memories—not many, but it's been a start, and he's been able to clear his conscience of you because he found himself married to you."

"But he *wants* to be married to me."

Louis was sure that was true, but he was also sure what Paul's reaction would be when Chris bravely and naively told him that she'd tricked him. He would be gone so fast they wouldn't even remember he'd been home. He, Louis, had to protect Chris from herself.

"Of course he does," he said brutally. "He has little choice at the moment. His Viper's at stake, and so is his reputation. Despite his disregard for public opinion, I doubt he'd want all of Eternity to know he'd abandoned you a second time."

Chris shook her head. She wasn't swallowing it. "That isn't why he's doing this. I know it isn't. He's come to love me."

"How do you know? You thought he loved you once before."

"Because I've truly come to love him. I thought I loved him once before, too, but that was very small compared to this. And I can't keep deceiving him." She turned her hand in his and grasped his apologetically. "I'm sorry, old friend, but I have to tell him. I won't be able to live with myself otherwise."

All right. Louis settled himself more comfortably in his chair. Time for the big guns. "I thought we were in this together. You're forgetting that you agreed to help *me* because of what I wanted out of this, as well as what you wanted."

"Louis..."

"Well, you may have assurances of his undying love, but I'm still just the old guy who drove away his mother and made his teen years unbearable."

"But you're getting on so much better. He took you sailing. He saved your life!"

Louis nodded. "That's right. I'm finally getting somewhere. Please don't destroy this for me before I've had a chance to reclaim my son."

Chris put a hand to her eyes and groaned.

Louis pressed his advantage. "I promise it won't be long," he said gently. "Trust me to see that everyone comes out a winner. Please. Don't say anything until I've had a chance to prepare him."

"I don't want you to tell him." Chris lowered her hand and met his gaze evenly. "I have to tell him. It has to come from me."

"Of course. Just let me tell you when."

"And it better not be long, because we've applied for the license, made an appointment with Bronwyn to try to get the chapel for next weekend, and he's asked Jacqui to look into getting us on a flight to Mexico for our honeymoon. You'd better be prepared to be best man!"

"Trust me," he said.

Chris studied him for a long moment, then finally fell back in her chair and nodded. "All right. But please make it soon. I feel so guilty, I'm sure it has to show."

Louis leaned toward her, warning gently, "Now come on. You started this as the consummate actress. You can continue a few more days. He's a reporter, remember. If you behave suspiciously, he'll see it. And if he sees it—it won't be long before he figures out what we've done. Then we're both dead in the water. You can do this, Christine."

"Right," she said flatly, picking up her cruller, looking at it in disgust and putting it down. "But be forewarned. Next time you go overboard, I'm not coming back for you."

"WHAT MAKES MEN so thickheaded?" Erica demanded as she shouldered her way into the shop, arms loaded with books, a colorful collection of pamphlets clutched in her hand.

Chris had to smile. Erica wore jeans today and a long, woven cotton shirt that looked like some giant's underwear, covered by a denim vest. A cord necklace with a cluster of bells hung to her waist.

Chris had been plagued with worry since her meeting with Louis, and she welcomed the distraction her volatile young friend provided.

"They have a higher level of concrete in their blood than we do," she replied, matching invoices to a billing statement. "Settles in their brains. Why?"

Erica went behind the counter to stuff her books into a slot reserved for their purses and possessions. "I thought Alex and I should talk to the travel agency to see what kind of honeymoon we can afford. I mean, I think we could do *something* if we knew how much to save. Well!" Her hands-up gesture suggested strongly that this idea hadn't met with the approval of some thickheaded male in her life. "You'd have thought I was planning a month in Europe! I mean, four days on the Vineyard, or maybe Nantucket or Marblehead. What could that cost?"

"Alex didn't like the idea?"

"Didn't like it? He went nuclear on me. He told me we had to stop thinking like kids and start considering savings accounts and money for a deposit on a house. Jeez! He's starting to sound like my dad!"

Chris patted her shoulder consolingly. "Well, he's right in a way. Life will change a lot for you when you're married. It costs so much more just to be alive than you could ever imagine. And if you want to think about buying a house one day, it's not too soon to start planning for it."

Erica tugged on her pendant of bells and asked imploringly, "But isn't a honeymoon important? Won't we get our marriage off to a better start if we have time alone together just to concentrate on each other? I mean, what's it going to do for us if we spend our wedding night going over the budget?"

Chris had to smile again. Erica, she thought, though still very young, showed all the signs of a survivor personality. Youth might get her into trouble, but her sheer determination and effervescent sense of humor would help her out.

But this was too important an issue in her friend's life for Chris to give her an easy answer.

"I can see both sides of this...." she began.

Erica raised both hands again and walked around the counter in exasperation. "Now *you* sound like my *mother*."

"An adult," Chris said evenly, "always listens to both sides. And a married woman at least listens to her husband's point of view before she goes off and does what she wants."

Erica smiled reluctantly. She leaned her elbows on the counter, the bells still clutched in her hand. "So, what's the other side?"

"The ugly truth," Chris said, feeling just a little like a fraud espousing truths about marriage when her own was just a role she'd slipped on. But Erica was important to her. She had to try. "I think four days on an island with the man you love is absolutely the best way to start a marriage. But if he's not in agreement, you'll both have a miserable time. And when you're married to Alex, you have to consider what he wants. And that responsibility begins the moment the priest declares you husband and wife. You can't just override him on honeymoon plans and decide to give him his say thereafter. It starts at the altar, Erica. Are you willing to compromise, or not?"

Erica straightened, frowning. "I don't know," she admitted crossly.

"Then it's a good thing you have a lot of time to think about this."

Erica glowered at Chris a moment, then looked around the shop and asked in confusion, "Then what is this all for? If marriage is just about rent and groceries, why bother with romantic stuff?"

Good question. Fortunately, in the past couple of weeks, Chris had learned a good answer. "Because when you and your husband are in agreement and working side by side to build a life together, these things add the spice that makes it fun."

"Fun?" Erica questioned doubtfully.

"Fun," Chris assured her.

Erica sighed exaggeratedly. "And I should trust your two weeks' experience in marriage?"

Chris grinned. "Have I ever given you bad advice?"

Erica rolled her eyes and ticked off on her fingers, "You tell me not to smoke, not to drink, not to take drugs and not to have sex." She placed her hands on her hips and went on. "Between you and my parents, I've become a social geek whose only satisfaction is double-fudge-brownie ice cream."

Chris reached under the counter and passed Erica a bottle of glass cleaner and a roll of paper towels. "We're only trying to save you from ruining your adulthood."

Erica snickered as she accepted the task. "Maybe, but you're sure messing up my senior year. The windows or the glass shelves?"

"Oh, I think you'll have to do both to work off all that frustration."

"MARRIED?" Louis pretended surprise. He sat beside his son on the stone bench in Carlotta's backyard. His landlady remained indoors, hard at work on refrigerator-cookie dough. "You're already married."

Paul gave one nod. He looked alive, Louis thought, as though his good looks had been somehow polished. There was a sheen about him that probably came from within, from the days he'd spent with Chris. The old remoteness was gone from his eyes—even when he looked at his father.

It did Louis's heart good to see that, and it reaffirmed his decision to withhold the truth about his scheme until the last possible moment—until Paul was in so deep nothing could harm what he felt for Chris, even the news that he'd been tricked into believing he'd married her.

"I want to be aware for this one," Paul said. "I want to know I got married. And I want Chris to know that I'm doing it willingly, even eagerly."

Louis raised an eyebrow. "What brought about this change of heart? Just the other day on the boat, you didn't know if you were staying or not."

"I guess I'm just slower than the average," Paul said, turning a gold-and-red oak leaf in his fingers. "I thought committing to someone caused you to risk something within yourself." He frowned at the leaf, but did not look up. "That's the way it's always happened before."

Louis knew he referred to his mother, and possibly to him, his father. In one case, he'd given love and watched Laurette walk away from it. In the other case, he'd given love and found its recipient selfish and unworthy.

"Twelve years ago," Paul went on, "I became afraid to love Christy because what she made me feel was so powerful. I didn't think I had myself together enough to handle it." He leaned back into the corner of the bench and tucked the oak leaf into the pocket of his flannel shirt. "I was too young to understand that love just has to be received and given back. That there's no magic formula, no set of steps to follow. If you can give openheartedly to the right woman, it comes back to you like a slot machine raining silver into the palm of your hand.''

Paul looked up at Louis at that, and his strong shoulders rose and fell in a thoughtful sigh. And Louis saw it for the first time, that faint suggestion in his son's eyes, the thought—not even big enough to be a suspicion—that made him wonder why his father didn't know that.

Louis held his breath, wondering if Paul would ask. He seemed to want to, but then he saw the small shake of his head that dismissed the impulse.

''So, I was wondering if you'd want to stand up for me,'' Paul said. ''You're already walking pretty well with the new cast.''

Another small step. Not the big one, but a move in the right direction all the same. Louis took the chance and put an arm around his shoulders. Paul didn't draw away.

''I'd be happy to. Does this mean I have to plan your bachelor party?''

Paul laughed. ''After what happened to me at the last one I attended, maybe not.''

''Nonsense,'' Louis insisted. ''I'll enlist Brent's help. You realize you'll lose your hero status among your friends for certain now?''

Paul accepted that with a wry nod. ''Interesting, isn't it, that it becomes more important to become a hero to a fragile woman than to a group of brawny men. I suppose that marks us as domesticated more than anything else.''

Louis clapped his shoulder. ''Marriage requires admiration and respect, as well as love.''

Paul gave him a quick glance at that statement, which probably sounded heretical coming from him. Louis awaited the quick swipe of his son's condemnation. It crossed his eyes, but it didn't come.

Paul stood to leave, giving Louis a hand up as he rose beside him. Slowly they walked across the green lawn to the arbor of ivy that led to the front.

"Would you look for a photo album for me?" Louis asked. "I think it's in the attic in that old trunk we used to keep at the foot of the bed."

Paul frowned at him. "You brought it with you from Jacqui's?"

Louis shook his head. "I've stored a lot of things in the attic, even while there were renters in the house. The place is so big, they never had a problem with storage, and I was so transient there for a while, that I just left everything there."

"Well, yeah. I guess. Do you need it right away?"

"In the next few days." He laughed softly. "There's a photo of you in there that I promised Chris."

Paul stood aside to let his father through the arbor. "If it's one of those naked-on-a-rug pictures, you can forget the whole thing."

Louis laughed again. "No. She's starting some kind of album for the two of you, and she thought you should both be represented from the very beginning. You don't mind?"

"Do I have right of final selection?"

"Of course not."

Paul smiled reluctantly. He rather liked the idea of his wife and his father in collusion over him. It made him feel comfortable somehow, surrounded. A feeling that would have made him run in terror only days ago.

"We'll see if I can find it first. Anything else you need?"

"Nope. That'll do it."

"Paul!" Carlotta came dashing down the front porch steps as Paul and Louis stood in front of the Viper. She held a large round tin in her hands, which she handed him. "I want you and Chris to test those for me, make sure my holiday goodies are up to snuff this year."

"It's only early October," Louis said.

Carlotta frowned at him. "There'll be cookies for the October church buffet, for the November bridge club and for my Thanksgiving dinner."

"That's another thing you have to be ready for," Louis said as Paul placed the tin on the passenger seat and slid behind the wheel. "They celebrate something all year long. Of course, you get to sample their menu, so it does have an up side."

Paul smiled at both of them. "Thank you, Carlotta. I'll be in touch, Dad."

"'Bye, son."

"Well." Carlotta hooked an arm in Louis's as they watched the sleek car speed down the quiet road. "Aren't you two getting on like gangbusters."

Louis nodded, a frown of concern chased by a considering smile. "Yes. I think he might even be ready to learn the truth about his mother."

Carlotta turned to him in surprise. "You're going to tell him?"

"In a way. I'm going to let him find out for himself." It was all in the album, and if Paul had the reporter's eye he was purported to have, he'd see it.

Carlotta kept a grip on Louis as he turned toward the house. "High time," she said. "High time."

PAUL WALKED into Chris's shop at closing time, locked the door after himself and turned the Closed sign.

"Customers around?" he asked in a low voice as he walked behind the counter.

Chris looked up from counting the day's receipts and saw the love and the passion in his eyes. Her concerns drained away from her as her heart responded.

"No," she said, reaching out a hand to him as he came within touching distance.

"Erica gone?"

"Yes."

"Good." With a grin, he leaned over her, pinning her to the cash register and kissed her senseless. The register rang and beeped and spewed an inordinately long length of tape.

They ignored it. Paul finally drew her away to look into her face. He saw love and happiness in her eyes and felt his own love and happiness expand astronomically.

He freed her and pointed to the neat bundles of cash, charge slips and reorder tags. "Almost done with that? We're going on a picnic."

She placed the money in a small safe, and the slips and tags in a file box to be taken back to her office.

"A picnic?" she asked. "At 6 p.m.? In early October?"

"Best time," he said, backing out from behind the counter as she reached for her purse and followed him. "The ants are asleep, and the outdoors aren't cluttered by sissy summer picnickers."

"Don't we need food?"

"We have it. Fried clams, coleslaw, cobs of corn and onion rings from Peabody's."

She let him out the door, then set the lock and the alarm. She stared at him in amazement as he caught her hand and led her toward the Viper. Wonderful aromas came from the floor on the passenger side where he'd stashed a duffel and a fat paper bag. She had to move a bottle of wine so she could sit in the passenger seat, then wedged her feet into a corner.

"You've thought of everything." She read the local but prestigious label, then held the bottle in her lap as she buckled her seat belt.

He winked at her as he settled in behind the wheel. "I guess some of you is rubbing off on me. Ready?"

"Yes. But where are we going?"

"The beach," he replied, and put the Viper in gear.

"It'll be closed."

"Not the Lafayette entrance. The north end where we don't have to deal with parking lots and locked gates. And the tide'll be out for a couple of hours."

"Ah." That end of the beach was too narrow to attract bathers and had always been a quiet spot.

A dark blue dusk had settled over everything by the time Paul led her to a cozy spot against a shallow bluff shaped like a crescent. She stood still in the middle of it while he gathered driftwood for a fire.

"This is where we used to come," she said, her voice quiet with wonder, "to talk about The Plan."

He built a ring of rocks and stacked wood in a pyramid. "That's right," he said, beckoning her to join him where he knelt. "Since it's finally going to happen after all these years, I thought we should discuss it here where it all began. Hold your coat open and give me some windbreak."

Chris complied and watched as the fire sparked, sputtered, climbed cautiously up a slender branch, then caught and lit the chunk of wood atop it.

Conscience tried to intrude, but she wouldn't let it. She couldn't sacrifice this moment on the altar of honesty. She just couldn't. Besides, what she felt for Paul was honest. The love she wanted to give him was honest. That should count for something.

He stood and pulled her back from the fire as it began to blaze.

"It was a very long day without you," he said, leaning down to tease her lips with his.

She turned away from all the warning signals and wrapped her arm around his waist, determined to have this time with him, to let Louis do what he had to do, then cope with the truth when the time came.

It occurred to her fleetingly that deceit grew bigger with each passing day, as did the difficulty of explaining it and the prospect of the reaction she could expect when she did. But she was becoming expert at a behavior she'd always despised in others—that of ignoring future consequences in the interest of immediate gratification.

She stood on tiptoe to return Paul's kiss. "I missed you, too," she said.

They sat against the bluff, Paul drew a blanket around them, and they opened the feast from Peabody's. Chris couldn't remember food ever tasting so delicious. The clams and onion rings had remained crispy on the short drive, the corn was sweet and succulent, and the coleslaw chunky and flavored with bits of pineapple. The wine was elegant and perfect.

Wind whipped around them, salty and exotically fragrant. The ocean, yards away, rushed toward them then receded in a musical riffle of sound. Farther down the beach, the surf crashed against the rocks on which the old lighthouse was built. The sound was powerful, like the crash of cymbals.

Other than the sounds of the water, the night was quiet. Road traffic was too far away to hear, and everyone else in Eternity was undoubtedly on his or her way home to eat indoors in a more traditional fashion. Chris pitied them.

Paul sipped at his wine, held Chris in the crook of his arm and absorbed the curious contentment. It was a new concept for him, but he found himself adjusting easily.

"Did you spend all day with the senior journalism class?" Chris asked. She held a fried clam up to him, and he bit it from her fingers.

He chewed and swallowed. "Most of the morning," he said. "Then I had lunch with them on the lawn, and we retired to the 'newsroom.'"

Chris nodded, remembering the classroom converted to look like a newspaper office, in which she and Paul had spent much of their senior year.

"They're so bright it scares me," he said with a small, self-deprecating laugh. "They have an intelligent grasp on what's going on in city government, they know school business inside out, even things they're not supposed to know, and they have a very lively sense of humor. You know what their big campaign is at the moment?"

"What?"

"Reforestation of the Alden Road woods."

Chris nodded against his chest. "A large part of it was cleared for a condo or something that never hap-

pened. Well, it's noble of them to think about putting
it back.''

He laughed softly. "No, it isn't. It's where they go
to *park.*''

"Really?'' She leaned away from him to look into
his eyes. In the encroaching darkness, they gleamed
with humor. "Don't they go to the old lace factory
anymore?''

"I guess now that it's condemned, the kids had to
find another spot. You have to admit the woods are
more romantic. And what do you know about the
factory? You'd never go with me." His voice grew
theatrically threatening. "Did you go with someone
else?''

Chris poked his shoulder. "Of course not. But
Anita did, and I got reports. You didn't forget dessert, did you? I mean, this just won't be the perfect
picnic feast without dessert.''

"I remembered that you have an insatiable sweet
tooth. Check my duffel.''

Chris sat up to reach for the army green, war-
surplus duffel that had contained their blanket.
Tucked deep in one end was a box of rolled wafers
with flavored centers—cappuccino.

"Yum," she said, pulling off the lid of the box. "I
suppose I have to share.''

"That's traditional in civilized societies.''

"I can be very *un*civilized where goodies are—
What on earth?''

"What?'' Paul leaned back lazily against the bluff,
both ends of the blanket now wrapped around him.

Chris strained to see in the firelight. She had reached
into the drum-shaped box for one of the cylindrical

cookies and pulled out two, which seemed to be stuck together. She moved her fingers down the length of the cookies and felt a narrow metallic object.

"The cookies are tied together," she said, knowing the words were absurd even as she said them. She scooted closer to the firelight.

"Who would do that?"

"I can't— Ah!" Chris's shriek was short and high-pitched.

"Problem?" Paul asked, still in that lazy tone.

In the glow from the fire, Chris studied the object that held the slender cookies together. It was a huge diamond solitaire on a gold band. She leaned closer still, unable to believe her eyes.

"I guess," she said softly, hesitantly, her voice trembling, "if a diamond can be considered a problem."

Paul took it from her, slipped the cookies out and dropped them on the box lid. He took her left hand and placed the solitaire on her finger, pushing it up against the wedding band. Then he brought her knuckles to his lips. "I love you, Christy. I know the diamond doesn't say it any more clearly, but it does sort of show how our love feels to me—deep and bright and precious."

Chris threw her arms around him and sobbed. Paul, thinking her simply overcome with emotion, drew her back from the fire and into the folds of the blanket. He held her between his knees, his cheek against hers.

"I have a great brownstone in Boston," he said, rocking her gently back and forth, "and there's a row of shops in the Charles Street area with a couple of empty spots. There's a Ben and Jerry's there. Perfect place for you to open a new Honeymoon Hideaway.'' He kissed her cheek as she continued to cry. ''When you're ready, we'll have a baby. If we do a good job and we like it, we'll have another. And we'll go to the Bahamas on our fifth anniversary, just like we've always planned. When we're old, we'll feed the pigeons on the Common, I'll wear a bolo tie, and you can dye your hair blue and we'll buy a camper and make our way across the country. Maybe we'll golf at Pebble Beach, then slowly make our way back home in time for Christmas with the grandkids. What do you think?''

She sobbed harder, her grip on his neck surprising him with its strength.

Taking that for approval of The Plan Revisited, he lay her down in the crook of his arm, pulled the blanket over them and unbuttoned her coat.

Chris refused to let her mind think. It wasn't difficult. She was so beset with emotion she was sure neither her brain nor her body could handle one more function.

Paul slipped a hand under her sweater and over her lace-covered breast, and she concentrated on this, knowing the reality of it would take her over, close off her awareness of everything else, make her forget her conscience and Louis, and the cruel trick they'd played on his son.

''Christy,'' Paul whispered as his lips replaced his hand.

Everything blurred for Chris but the touch of Paul's mouth on the tip of her breast. Desire rose hot and strong as he planted kisses between her ribs and downward.

She pulled at his jacket as he lifted her shirt, and she gasped at the delicious touch of his palm against her hip. He slipped his hand inside her panties, an expert flick of his wrist drew them down.

Chris undid the button of his slacks and dealt with the zipper. She tugged at the twill waistband, wondering how to free him from it without disturbing the blanket that covered them. But in no time it ceased to be a problem. He was inside her, filling her, calling up immediately that maddening, tightening spiral that ruled her world while it lived. Delicious fulfillment came, accompanied by the smell of the ocean, the rasp of the sand, the softness of a velour blanket that was the only thing between them and the night.

Paul was relieved that she'd stopped crying, and he credited their lovemaking as the powerful force that distracted her from her tears. She'd always been emotional. The night of their prom, when they'd talked on the bridge about marriage, she'd wept in his arms.

But these tears had been a little unsettling. He knew they were an expression of love. He could see it in her eyes, feel it in the touch of her hands, in her body's response to him.

Even now, as she shuddered in his arms, he sensed that her passion was mingled with tears. She clung to him as though he was all she wanted in this world. And that sent him over the edge into his own ecstasy.

When they were quiet again, he felt her damp eyelashes flutter against his shoulder. "I love you, Paul," she whispered, her voice hoarse and quiet. "I love you."

The words reassured him to his very soul. He kissed her and pulled her coat closed. "I love you, too, Christy."

She reached up to help him pull his sweater and T-shirt down, and scratched his ribs with the diamond solitaire.

Chapter Eleven

"So Saturday's all right with you?" Paul asked for the third time as they drove to the Powell chapel.

"I thought I already answered that," Chris said with a casual tone that even she had to marvel at. At the moment, her entire concentration was riveted on how to deal with Bronwyn when Paul explained that they wanted to be married a second time.

She would be bound to ask him who'd married them the first time. What would she, Chris, do when Paul replied, "Why, you did, Bronwyn," and Bronwyn frowned at him in perplexity and said, "But I didn't, Paul. You must be mistaken." Now. She had to tell him the truth now. But she'd promised Louis. She prayed for divine intervention.

No one was more surprised than Chris when her prayers were answered. Intervention came in the form of Patience, sitting in for her niece for the afternoon.

"She's feeling a little under the weather today," Patience explained, smiling from ear to ear as Paul explained about their wedding. "So Violet's sitting in my shop and I'm just doing office duty here, answering the phone and handling the schedule. What a wonderfully romantic idea, Paul." She gave him a ju-

licious but maternal glance as she consulted the big
book. "I understand you don't remember much about
the first wedding. Well, actually, I guess it was the
second wedding, but the first one doesn't count because you weren't here for it."

Patience looked distressed to have expressed that
thought aloud, and she buried her nose in the book.

Chris held her breath. Paul said nothing about their
previous wedding, and Patience, bless her, didn't ask.
She simply found Saturday in the book, glanced at the
appointments and said, "Ten's free on Saturday."

Paul turned to Chris. "Ten o'clock's fine," she said
with a weak smile.

"Good." Patience penciled in the appointment.
"So, Chris, your third wedding will be at 10 a.m. on
Saturday. It's down in black and white."

My third wedding, Chris thought. She was beginning to feel like some female Bluebeard, only the same
man had been involved every time. And she hadn't
killed him. The first time she'd just boxed him in a
corner and the second time she'd tricked him. This
time, she was going to have to lay a heavy truth on him
he wasn't going to like. She put a hand to a pain in the
region of her heart.

The chapel office door burst open and Erica, who
was supposed to be watching the Hideaway, walked in
with Alex. They seemed to be in the middle of an argument.

"But it's only October," Alex was saying. He was
dressed in shorts and a hooded sweatshirt. "Why are
we setting a date now for something that won't happen till next July?"

Erica turned to him impatiently. "I've *told* you!
Because everyone comes to Eternity to get married,

particularly in the summer, and we have to reserve a date now if we want to have it."

"It's nine months away," Alex declared.

Erica, more agitated than Chris had ever seen her, said, "But plans *have* to be made. Do you want to do this or not?"

Alex turned with athletic agility and left the office. Erica watched him go as though she couldn't believe her eyes. Then she turned to Patience and noticed Paul and Chris for the first time. She joined her hands together and squared her shoulders, a poignant picture of wounded pride and dignity. Through the office window, Chris saw Alex jog away.

"I'm sorry," she said to everyone in general, then she focused on Chris, looking uncomfortably guilty. "I'm sorry about the shop. I just closed it for a few minutes because this was the only time I could get Alex to come with me." Her voice was high and fragile. "I'm heading right back."

"Why don't you take the morning off?" Chris suggested, going to her and putting an arm around her. "We're finished here, so I'll take care of the shop."

Erica shook her head. "Thanks. But I'm going back. And you're supposed to be making your own wedding plans. Mine are probably history." Her chin began to tremble, but she drew a steadying breath. "Don't hurry back. See you later."

"Oh, dear, oh, dear," Patience said when the door closed behind the girl. "That doesn't look good, does it?"

Paul went to Chris, who stared worriedly after Erica, running to her little red Toyota. "She probably shouldn't be alone," he said. "I'll take you to the shop, then I'll arrange for the flowers and the photographer."

Chris turned to him, momentarily distracted from concern for Erica by her own problems. "Paul, all I need is a small bouquet, and a photographer is such an expense. I'm sure Brent will take pictures." *Presuming, of course, that this does happen once you know the truth,* she finished silently.

"I'll take care of it," he said. "Come on. Thank you, Patience."

Patience waved cheerfully from behind the desk. "Good luck, kids. Third time's a charm."

CHRIS FOUND ERICA restocking the film rack and sobbing uncontrollably. Paul had stopped for café mochas on the way, and Chris drew her assistant into the chair behind the counter and forced one into her hand.

When she tried to resist, Chris insisted. "It's raspberry, just the kind you like. Drink it. You'll feel better."

"I'll never feel better," Erica said. She put the mocha aside, folded her arms and settled into a deep despair. "I don't know what's happening."

Chris pulled over the step stool and sat facing Erica. "I think you do," she said gently. "If you give it a little thought, you'll see what's happening."

Erica looked at her suspiciously, eyes wet and hurt. "He doesn't care about this," she said, a trace of anger overtaking her grief. "That's what's happening. Did you see the way he was dressed to make wedding plans? He had to fit me in before football practice."

"What does that tell you?"

Erica's face crumpled. "I know. I've had college prep psychology. He didn't want to be there, and he didn't know how to tell me. So the best he could do was *show* me what his priorities are!"

Chris held her while she wept, something so familiar about all of it. She had to make certain Erica understood what she, Chris, hadn't twelve years before.

She took Erica's mocha off the counter and forced it on her a second time. "Drink that," she said, "and let me explain the rest of it to you."

Erica removed the lid and took a sip of the fragrant brew, every gesture heavy with despair. "What 'rest of it'? I'm trying to put together a wedding the groom is panicking about."

"Erica, there are nine months until July," Chris said reasonably.

"I know." Erica rolled her eyes in frustration. "But I wanted to have a date—"

"So you could tie it all up, make it firm," Chris asked quietly, "because you could see him pulling away? Did you think if you made appointments all over Weddings, Inc., that would somehow guarantee for you that you'd have a wedding?"

Erica sipped her mocha, then leaned back in the chair. She sniffed and admitted grimly, "Yeah, I think so. It scared me to see him losing interest when the idea of getting married just seemed better and better to me." She sipped more coffee and added sadly, "I guess I just don't understand *why* he grew to love me less when I just love him more and more."

"I don't think he loves you less, Erica," Chris said, propping her feet on the bottom of the stool and wrapping her arms around her knees. "It's just that, as a rule, men prefer to be less...structured than women prefer. And trying to tie them down to times and dates and general fuss makes them want to escape."

Erica shook her head, clearly confused. "I don't understand. When I talked about a honeymoon, all he could think about was budgets and bank accounts—all the practical, structured things in marriage. But when I tried to plan the fun part of it, the wedding itself, he didn't want to be pinned down. It doesn't make sense."

"To a man, it does." Chris laughed. "A responsible man feels as though he has to take charge of the parts of marriage that require order and self-discipline, and when he can't see his way clear to doing that, all the rest of it becomes just so much aggravation—even the part that should be fun."

"But Alex is usually very organized. Why does he think marriage is going to be so tough?"

This was the hard part. Chris tried to approach it gently. "Possibly because his journalism career is more important to him than you realize. He loves you. I'm convinced he does. But he wants something for himself he knows goes against what you want right now. And he doesn't know how to tell you, so—just as you said about his wearing his football practice clothes this morning—unconsciously, he tried to show you."

Erica nodded. "But he can't afford to go to college."

"He could afford to go to junior college if he didn't have to support a wife."

"But I'll be working, too. And my father promised him a good job with lots of benefits."

"I know. It sounds to you as if it makes perfect sense. But it doesn't to him. And that's something you can't ignore. Unless you want to drive him away completely—or unless you want to have a miserable marriage."

Erica downed a large gulp of mocha and sniffed again. "Maybe I'll join the Israeli army," she said. "They're men who appreciate women."

Chris shook her head. "My idea of equality is not the front line in combat."

"Why not?" Erica asked with a wide, questioning gesture of her arms. Mocha sloshed in her cup. "Is love any different? It certainly doesn't hurt any less than having your foot shot off."

"Ever had your foot shot off?"

Erica did not appreciate the teasing. "No, I haven't, but you know what I mean."

Chris stood and put an arm around her shoulders. "Yes, I do. But you have to step back and take a look at what's happening here. First of all, summer is more than half a year away, and both you and Alex can change a great deal in that time. If you did decide to put the wedding off for a little while, what's the worst that could mean? You could take a few courses at the community college yourself and still work part-time here. Or you could get a full-time job, save your money and have all kinds of options if you decide against marriage, after all, or a good nest egg if you decide for it. Taking time usually doesn't hurt anything, Erica."

"But I had such plans," she said urgently, with the same eagerness to employ them Chris remembered having at that age. "I thought if we started out together with great enthusiasm, there isn't anything we can't do."

Chris nodded, then reminded her gravely, "That was what I thought when I was in your place. I pushed for it, and look at what happened to me. Don't make the same mistake."

Erica sighed, downed the rest of her mocha, crumpled the cup and tossed it into the trash. She stood decisively. "I'll finish the film rack. Then I'll straighten up the cards and the paperbacks. I'm sorry about closing the shop, but it was the only time Alex had, and I was afraid not to take it. I wasn't thinking straight."

Chris nodded. "It's all right. Men are enough to make the most together woman crazy."

"Thanks. Did you get your wedding plans all made?"

Chris's smile faltered slightly as she shifted Erica's problems aside and confronted her own. "Mostly. Paul was going to take care of the flowers and the photographer this afternoon."

Erica smiled wistfully. "That's great. You're really going to put on a big production. Doesn't it make you feel wonderful that he wants to do that?"

Erica had no way of knowing, of course, that all his enthusiasm for their remarriage did was twist the knife in an already painful wound. So Chris smiled brightly and nodded. "Wonderful. I'll get that box of gift cards from the office."

PAUL LEANED against the kitchen counter, took a large bite out of a crunchy red apple and considered the photo album he'd finally located in the attic. He'd brought it downstairs, intent on simply putting it in the car and taking it to Carlotta's. But something about it nagged at him.

The album contained pictures of his mother. He hadn't opened it yet, but he remembered that before things had gone bad between his parents, he'd watched over his mother's shoulder as she'd pasted pictures in it. He remembered photos of school field trips his mother had chaperoned. Cub Scout functions where Louis had served as an assistant to the Scoutmaster. Birthday parties, parades, vacations.

He took another bite of apple, but moved no closer to the table. Much of his past was contained in that album—the part of it he'd chosen to forget when it had been clear his mother wasn't coming back.

He was over it now, of course. He was adjusted. That had been such a short span of years, and the future was now spread before him, filled with hope and happiness. He had so much more than he'd ever anticipated.

He didn't have to touch those years ever again. But he did. They poked and prodded at him like a toothache. A comfortable future required a past rid of old baggage. And he'd acquired a new courage since he'd fallen in love with Christy all over again.

He went to the table. He put a fingertip to the simple brown leatherette cover that said Photos in gold embossing and opened it.

His parents smiled up at him from their wedding picture, his mother dark and slight and serious, Louis tall and erect and smiling broadly. Paul pulled out a chair and sat down.

PAUL WAS ON THE SOFA when Chris walked in with a bag filled with cartons of Chinese food. The photo album was open on the coffee table, and he stared at it, elbows resting on his knees, hands crossed over his mouth.

Louis had called her at the shop that afternoon to assure her again that everything would be fine, that she had only to continue the charade another day or two and the deception she'd grown to hate would be over. She had to trust him. He'd told her, also, not to be surprised if Paul mentioned the photographs he'd told him she'd requested. He'd asked for her cooperation in pretending she knew all about it.

She saw Paul poring over the album.

There was a strange tension in him, a deep absorption she suspected was part of Louis's curious request. There was something in the album, she suspected, Louis had wanted Paul to see.

"Hi." Chris put the bag on the coffee table, pulled her coat off and sat beside Paul on the sofa. He placed an arm around her without looking up from the album.

Chris leaned into him, forgetting all tricks and manipulations. She was aware only that he seemed distressed, and she wanted to help. "What's up?" she asked cautiously. "Reminiscing?"

He frowned and rubbed her shoulder. "Rediscovering is more like it." Then he removed his arm from around her and turned back a few pages. "Dad said you wanted a photo of me as a kid for something you're doing for the wedding."

"Yeah." Her tone was noncommittal.

"So I dug out the album and was going to take it to him. But I couldn't resist looking inside."

"Of course not. Who doesn't love old photographs? And that was a good time of your life, wasn't it? I mean, before your parents broke up?"

Paul nodded, one hand still pensively over his mouth while the other pointed to a photograph. It was of a cabin in the woods, with Paul as a child about eight in hiking clothes, his mother and father on either side of him, similarly dressed. Off to the right, near their car, was a tall, well-built man with indistinguishable features.

"Do you recognize him?" Paul asked.

Chris leaned over the album for a closer look. The muscular body would have made the man memorable even if one had never seen his face. But he wasn't familiar to Chris.

"No. Do you?"

Paul nodded, still staring at the photo. "His name was Owen Hamilton. He was a friend of my father's."

Chris nodded. "Is that important?"

"I think so." Paul pointed to several more photographs on the next few pages. "He's in many of these. As I recall, he worked with my father when he ran the dinner theater here in Eternity for a couple of years. He had the small acting company that performed there."

He must have spent a lot of time with Paul's family, Chris concluded. He was in almost every photo that spanned several years of the Bertrands' lives. Sometimes he was accompanied by a young woman, never the same one, but usually he existed singly on the fringe of their lives, an image in the corner of every photo, lounging against a road sign, on a picnic blanket, against a cabin porch.

Paul turned another page. "Now, look at this one."

Chris leaned closer. The photograph had been taken on the wharf, and the central figures in it were Paul and his father, proudly displaying a fish they'd caught.

Off to the side, probably considering themselves out of the frame, were Paul's mother and Owen Hamilton. They weren't touching, but they looked into each other's eyes, obviously unaware of the grinning man and boy. They had eyes only for each other, and it would have taken a blind person, Chris thought, to miss the sexual message in their gaze.

"I remember that day," Paul said, his voice quiet and heavy. "Dad and I had a great time. I caught the fish and considered myself quite the hero. I remember that my mother and Owen spent all the time we were fishing inside the cabin of the boat. In my innocence, I thought they were drinking coffee or talking." He shook his head and leaned against the back of the sofa. "This was a good two years before my mother left."

Chris wrapped her arms around his neck. He curved an arm around her waist, his eyes still on the album. "Why would she have mounted that photograph," he asked, "when what it reveals is so obvious?"

Chris stroked the back of his neck where the muscles were tense and hard. "It's hard to say from this distance," she replied, unwilling to voice the obvious answer.

"What's your best guess?" He turned to look at her, his eyes dark and knowing.

She sighed and held him a little tighter. "I'd say she was out to hurt your father."

Paul nodded. "Hamilton's the man she left with two years later."

Chris felt Paul sink slightly into the sofa as though something had gone out of him. She kissed his cheek and rested hers on his shoulder. "So they'd been having an affair for some time. She wasn't the woman you idealized, but then, your father wasn't the villain you imagined, either. So it evens out a little, doesn't it?"

"He never told me."

"He knows how much you loved her. He didn't want to hurt you any more than you'd been hurt already."

Paul knew he shouldn't feel anger. He should feel guilt, remorse, self-recrimination that, as an adult, he'd never looked back to examine that part of his life and find the truth. He'd been too content with knowing whom to blame.

He got to his feet and paced the living room, edgy and mad as hell. He turned for the door. "I'm going to see him."

"Wait!" Chris intercepted him, her hands on his forearms. "You can't confront him in this mood. It isn't fair."

"Fair?" Paul demanded. "Was it fair to let me grow up under a misapprehension?"

"The misapprehension," she said gently, "was that the mother you loved was sweet and faithful, and that your father was the villain of the piece. Don't you see what you're doing?"

He folded his arms, impatient with her analysis. "What am I doing?"

"You're reacting the way I did. It's hard for you to see that Louis isn't a monster, after all. Just like it was hard for me to see that you weren't the villain I'd painted in my mind. Only I had you to beat up to relieve my frustration." She pulled his folded arms loose and caught his hands in hers. "But you can't beat up on your father to relieve yours. He's considerably older and has a broken leg."

Chris looped her arms around Paul's neck. "You can't go over there tonight feeling angry. Go in the morning when you've had time to think about it and can see that he was loving you, not hurting you, by keeping that secret."

Paul's anger dissolved as his determination to have it out with Louis fell victim to Chris's tender gaze.

"Tonight you need to be loved, to be reminded that, whatever happened in the past, Louis has always loved you, and so have I."

Paul took her in front of the fire in a tangle of emotion so complex he didn't even try to sort it out. A moment ago the burden of having mistaken his father's intentions all these years weighed on him like a yoke. But Chris's words and the touch of her hands as she pulled off his shirt, helped him with her jeans, pushed him onto his back and rose over him made his confusion disappear.

Love. Truth focused with the precision of a laser right to the center of his being. His life was filled with it now, apparently had been for longer than he'd realized. What had happened didn't matter. His father had handled it out of love. And the woman he, Paul, had abandoned as a confused young man loved him still, would love him always.

Chris took him inside her and he groaned with pleasure as she enclosed him and began to move in the primal circle that was the path of everything in the universe.

Firelight gleamed in her hair, burnished her cheeks, her breasts and the small curve of her stomach. He cupped his hands over her breasts and felt their supple warmth. The feel of her beaded nipples against his palms somehow loosened what remained of his tension and made him smile.

She returned the smile, caught his hands and kissed them. Then she laced her fingers with his and used their leverage to raise and lower herself over him.

It was only a matter of seconds before he pulled free of her hands, bracketed her waist to hold her still and erupted inside her with all the turbulence of his discovery, but also with the well of tenderness he'd found within himself that seemed to grow deeper day by day.

Chris collapsed on top of him, pushing away all thought. Her love for Paul was so powerful, so critical to her well-being, that she would let nothing take it from her. At this moment she preferred to forget that anything even threatened to try.

Chapter Twelve

"She was having an affair with Hamilton," Paul said, "long before you had the affair that made her leave."

He sat with his father in a pair of wicker chairs on Carlotta's screened-in front porch. For today, at least, the golden autumn had given way to a noisy, torrential rain. It drummed on the roof, hissed on the sidewalk, puddled in the grass and made everything beyond look as though seen through a frosted window.

The album stood on the wicker table between them, but neither of them had opened it.

Louis turned to Paul, looking tired and less like the old roué everyone knew and loved, despite his reputation.

"I thought if you saw the photos as an adult, you'd see what I couldn't tell you."

Paul stared out at the rain, unable to understand why his father had let his wife's affair go on so long.

"Why did you tolerate it?" he asked. "Judging by that one photo, it must have gone on for some time. It was two years after that that she left."

Louis sighed heavily, thinking this wasn't as cleansing as he'd imagined it would be. It still hurt, after all these years, and he couldn't read Paul's reaction.

"You may find this difficult to believe," Louis admitted with a laugh at himself that had little to do with humor, "but I never suspected. I loved her. I trusted him. I thought they were good friends—that all three of us were good friends. Then I overheard someone talking at a party. Apparently your mother and Owen had disappeared together to the boathouse, and everyone had noticed but me."

Louis pulled the wool jacket he wore more tightly around him and frowned in the direction of the album, his gaze unfocused. "I slipped out to the woods at the back of the house and watched the boathouse. They came out together laughing and straightening their clothes."

Paul saw remembered pain in his father's eyes and reached out to touch his sleeve.

"Did you confront her?"

Louis nodded. "She promised to end it, but I guess she was just more in love with him than she was with me."

Paul heard in his father's voice that he'd had difficulty accepting that truth. "She made time for you, but never for me. So...I had a woman-friend who was kind." His gaze at Paul was apologetic. "Of course, I knew that wasn't the way to handle it, but I was lonely, and I think I wanted to hurt your mother back, too."

"Why didn't you just leave?"

Louis met his son's eyes, wondering if he would believe him. Then he decided it didn't really matter. It was true.

"Because that would have meant leaving you. And you were so bright, so warm and interested in everything. And you loved *her* so much. I didn't know what to do."

Paul took a moment to swallow. "Why did she finally leave?"

"I believe it was Owen's ultimatum. He'd gotten a job off-off Broadway and he wanted her to go with him."

Paul had to ask the question. Had determined when he drove over this morning that he would ask the question. But now it stuck in his throat, its potential to hurt him more of a reality than he'd realized. His throat ached. But he had to know.

"Why did she leave me?"

This time, Louis took hold of Paul's arm, his eyes filled with misery and apology. "Because Owen wanted her, but he didn't want you."

"And she wanted him," Paul made himself admit, "more than she wanted me."

"The world," Louis said, his voice rough, his hand tightening on Paul's arm, "is full of people who do stupid things out of self-interest. I'm sorry, but I was grateful she left you. I could never have kept you from her because you loved her so much, but I love you, too."

Rain slashed across the porch steps, washing everything in its path.

Paul swallowed the truth and felt his throat relax. He'd probably suspected it all along but hadn't wanted to know it for a fact until Chris had finally shown him what real love was.

"You should have told me," Paul grumbled half-heartedly.

Louis shrugged a shoulder, his eyes brimming with unshed tears. "I know. I just couldn't hurt you that way. It was easier to let you hurt me."

"Dad," Paul scolded, and reached out of his chair to pull the old man to him.

Louis wept. Paul swallowed.

"Son." Louis drew away after a moment, knowing the time had come for complete truth.

"Yes?"

Louis opened his mouth to explain what he'd done with loving intentions, what had come out precisely as he'd planned—then he remembered he'd promised Chris he would let her explain.

He closed his mouth reluctantly, shook his head and tried again while Paul waited with patient interest.

"Sometimes," Louis said finally, "we do things that appear unkind because...well, because we're not brilliant strategists. We're just people doing our best to bring about..."

Paul stopped his rambling with a nod and a brief smile. "I understand, Dad. I do."

But he didn't. He couldn't.

Louis called Chris the moment Paul was out the door.

"HE LEFT just a few minutes ago." Chris, standing in the middle of the kitchen with a wooden spoon in one hand, held the phone in a white-knuckled grip with the other and listened to Louis's emotional voice. "He...told me he loved me," he said. "He held me."

"Louis," Chris whispered. It was the long-awaited step forward out of the tangle. But the next step would determine the rest of her life. She was about to tell Paul the truth. Would he understand and accept what she'd done as he'd accepted his father's actions? She found it impossible to speculate. Paul never reacted the way she expected.

"I could come over," Louis offered, "and explain that it was all my—"

"No." Chris raised her wooden spoon like a scepter. "I have to tell him myself. It wasn't all your fault. Had I said no in the beginning, your scheme would have died. I'm the one who was eager to participate, who played the role of his wife so convincingly that even the jaded reporter in him believed me. I'm the one who made him fall in love."

"And who fell in love herself."

"Yes. Was he heading right home?"

Louis's voice took on an edge of concern. "He was stopping to meet Brent at the inn for a drink. Chris, are you sure this is the best way...?"

"Yes. I'll call you later. After I've told him, we'll all have to talk."

"If you're sure."

"I'm sure. Thank you, Louis."

Thank you. The ironic words hung in the air as Chris cradled the receiver. Thank you for giving me the chance to implement my own plan for revenge? For letting me see what I've missed all these years, what life could be like as his wife? For letting me experience the wonder of having Paul as deeply in love with me as I've always been with him? For terrifying me with the prospect that Paul will hate me for what I've done and never want to see me again?

Chris walked resolutely back to the carrot-cake mixture she'd been pouring into a pan and refused to consider that final thought. Paul would understand. He would. As she placed the pan in the oven, she ignored the overpowering fear that she was kidding herself.

"I'M GLAD you straightened it all out with Louis," Brent said. He and Paul were sitting at the far end of the ornate mahogany bar in the inn's lounge. "He's a good old guy. And it's easier to have a wedding when everyone's on good terms."

Brent raised his glass of dark beer. "To women. What *would* we have without them?"

Paul laughed lightly, raising his mineral water. He felt vaguely disoriented after that conversation with his father, and he didn't need alcohol to blur the edges of an already out-of-focus reality.

"Really," he said. "What do we need with freedom and peace of mind, anyway?"

"Don't even remember what those are. I'll pick you up for the party tomorrow night. And maybe I'd better pick you two up the morning of the wedding. You can't stuff the bride into the passenger seat of the Viper."

"Good point. We'd appreciate that."

"Got the cruise tickets?"

"Yeah. Christy still thinks we're flying. I'm going to enjoy surprising her."

"Surprisssing . . . who?" The question was slurred, the words separated as though they could only be considered one at a time.

Paul and Brent turned to find Danny Tucker standing behind them, a hand on each of their shoulders. He was wearing a suit and tie, the tie pulled away from his throat, his eyes bleary and bloodshot.

"Danny," Paul said in concern, turning on the stool to steady him with a hand on his shoulder. "You'd better sit down, buddy, before you fall down."

Danny nodded agreeably as Paul and Brent supported him while they crossed the room to a booth. "Had a . . . little too-oo much. Wife three-eew me out. Surprissse . . . who?"

"Chris," Brent said. "Paul and Chris are getting married day after tomorrow."

Danny looked at Paul vacantly. Brent asked the bartender to pour a cup of coffee.

"You're ree-ealy . . . going to marry her this time?" Danny asked, his bleary eyes blinking in confusion.

Paul slipped into the booth opposite him. "Yep. This time I'm going to show up for my wedding. Relax, Danny. You'll feel better when we get some coffee in you."

Danny shook his head, and his eyes seemed to roll. He blinked again and tried to focus on Paul as Brent placed the cup of steaming coffee before him. "You're gonna marry her after . . . after what she did?"

Paul and Brent stared at him. "I'm the one who never made it to the church," Paul said.

Danny shook his head again. "Not that time. Last time. *She* didn't make it to the church. Nobody did. It didn't . . . happen."

There was a moment's stunned silence. Then Brent stood suddenly and tried to pull Danny out of the booth. "Come on, pal. I'll get you home. I think you're a danger to yourself in this—"

"No." Paul caught Brent's arm and removed it from Danny. "Leave him alone." He turned his attention to the man who raised the coffee cup with shaky hands. "What do you mean, Dan?" he asked calmly.

"I mean..." He put the cup down, then put a hand to his head, his brow furrowing as he tried to think. "Ah—I think . . . I'm not supposed to say."

Paul placed a hand over Danny's other wrist and applied just enough pressure to penetrate the drunken haze. "It's all right to tell me," he said. "I don't remember that night. Do you?"

A dark suspicion was forming in the back of Paul's mind. He felt everything inside him slow as he waited for Tucker to speak.

"No," Danny said vaguely, "becaussse . . . nothing happened. No wedding." He stared, his eyes troubled but unfocused. Then he looked at Brent. "Was there?"

Paul turned to Brent, his eyes demanding. "Was there?" he asked quietly.

Brent shook his head, his expression grim. "I don't know. I remember that you left the party to look for Louis's medication, and when you came back about an hour later, you had Chris with you and you told us you were getting married."

Paul pointed to Danny. "Where was he? Why does he think it didn't happen?"

Brent opened his mouth as though to reply, then shook his head.

"Why?" Paul demanded flatly.

Brent sighed and rubbed a hand over his forehead. "As I remember, Louis came back into the party and called him out sometime before you came back. But we were all under the influence of partying and bemoaning our fates. I could be wrong."

"No," Danny said with sudden lucidity. "No. There was no wedding. I remember because I made a phony...a phony...you know. With my notary seal."

"License," Paul said, remembering the morning he'd awakened and found himself married to Christy—or thought he was. He'd gone into the bathroom and found the document on the mirror. Very legal and convincing.

"License," Danny confirmed with a shaky nod. "But no wedding. Weird. I told 'em it was weird, but Chris said it wasn't—that it was payback."

Paul heard the word—payback. It reverberated in his mind like a shriek. Then it stopped and he heard the sound of his life ripping apart. Deep anger and acute pain rose in him with a force that brought him to his feet.

Brent stood to let him out of the booth, but tried to stop him with a hand on his arm. Paul shook him off and slapped a bill on the table. First his mother, now his wife. Except that she'd never really been his wife. Pain swelled inside him with barbed edges.

"Get him home," he said, and walked out of the lounge, through the brightly lit foyer of the restaurant and out into the dark gray downpour.

CHRISTY TURNED OFF the oven, which had been keeping dinner warm, and put the carrot cake in the refrigerator. Her movements were calm, but panic bubbled up inside her like a geyser.

Paul knew. Louis had called shortly after two o'clock and it was now almost eight and Paul hadn't returned home or called. She doubted that anything short of an accident would have kept him away without calling, and she'd checked out that possibility with the police more than an hour ago.

She didn't know how it had happened or why, but she knew he'd found out. And the fact that he hadn't come home to confront her was not a good sign.

She'd lost him again.

She heard a knock at the door. Knowing Paul wouldn't knock, she ran to it, her heart pounding as she wondered if she'd been wrong about an accident, after all.

But it was Alex who stood on the porch, hands jammed in the pockets of his jacket, his face pale, his jaw squared in a look of adult resolution. The moment his eyes settled on Chris's face, his whole demeanor seemed to collapse.

"Is Paul home?" he asked in a weak voice. Beyond the porch, rain fell in a thick sheet.

Chris shook her head. "I'm sorry. He's out."

Alex sighed. "Then, can I talk to you for a minute, Chris?"

Chris fought disappointment. She didn't want to talk to Alex now. She wanted to talk to Paul. But Paul was probably gone, and Alex stood on her doorstep looking like a broken young man.

She pushed aside her own fears and regrets with an almost physical force and smiled at Alex as she stepped aside to let him in.

"Want a soda?" she asked, trying to take his jacket. "Cocoa?"

He held the sides of the jacket firmly in his hands as he shook his head. "Thanks, but I won't be here that long. I just have to... explain to you what happened in case Erica..." His brow furrowed and she swore his lip trembled. "In case I don't see her again."

Her own problems now really put aside, Chris led him to the sofa and sat him down. "All right, Alex. I'm listening."

Alex leaned against the back of the sofa, hesitating a moment as his eyes seemed to focus on what had happened. Then he shook his head and said grimly, "I can't believe I did this."

A dozen possibilities crossed Chris's mind, most of which were impossible to equate with the bright and courteous young man sitting on her sofa. So she waited for him to explain.

He shook his head and met her gaze. "Erica offered to go to the Alden Road Woods with me," he said. "To have sex."

He folded his arms and put a hand over his face for a minute, then dropped it. "And I said no. Do you believe that? I said no. Me. I said no."

Chris's immediate reaction was sympathy for both of them—for Erica, who was desperate enough to make the suggestion, and for Alex, who lived in a world and among peers who made him feel diminished for having refused.

"You were right, Alex," she told him. "You know you were."

His blue eyes were doubtful. "She told me I'm a wishy-washy indecisive creep, and she never wants to see me again, much less marry me. I tried to make her understand what Paul told me about style...."

Chris's eyebrows rose. "Style?"

"Yeah," Alex went on. "He said love shapes your whole life and that success and fortune mean nothing if you don't have someone who loves you to share it with you. He said that loving a woman with style is the most important thing a man ever does." Alex shook his head and expelled an exasperated breath. "But she wouldn't listen. I know I hurt her feelings, but I thought if I explained, she'd understand that I want to make love with her more than I want anything, but I'm trying to make sure that when we get together, we'll stay together."

Pain vibrated through Chris's being at the knowledge that she'd deceived a man who felt that way. "I didn't know he understood that," she said almost to herself.

"He says he learned it when he was separated from you." Alex smiled grimly and sat forward. "You're lucky that you're both mature enough to know what you're doing. That you've finally figured it all out." He stood. "Thanks for listening. Maybe you can explain it all to her better than I did. I guess I can live with it if she never wants to see me again. I just want her to know I did it because I love her, not because I don't."

Chris followed him to the door, smiling wisely, pretending that things were precisely as he thought they were. She was getting frighteningly good at deception.

As she waved him off, the Viper turned into the driveway, picking out the rippling sheet of rain in its headlights. Heart pounding, blood pumping, she remained where she was as Paul turned off the ignition and the lights and opened the car door.

Maybe I'm wrong, she told herself with a feeble burst of hope. *Maybe he got talking with Brent and forgot the time.*

Paul leapt out of the car with a bouquet of flowers and ran for the porch. Chris's little burst of hope swelled, pushing her fears to a far corner of her heart. She'd jumped to conclusions. He *didn't* know.

"Hi!" she said, raising her arms to him. "I was getting worried."

"Were you?" He caught the back of her neck in one hand and lowered his mouth to hers. At the last moment she saw the banked fury in his eyes and tried to draw back. But she was too late. Hope rushed out of her as though he'd severed an artery that contained it. He *did* know.

Chris stiffened against the expected assault of his mouth. He would punish her with this kiss.

But he didn't. He was gentle, even tender, coaxing her stiff lips apart, invading her softness, taunting her with artful forays of his tongue, then drawing up a response that dropped her defenses and confused her completely.

Her head lolled back against his arm when he finally drew away. "Paul..." she began.

Satisfaction slid over the fury in his eyes, confusingly out of place with his tenderness. Until he dropped his arms from her with a finality that made everything suddenly very clear. She realized the sweetness of the kiss was her punishment—because, judging by the implacable line of his jaw, she would never experience it again.

He marched before her into the house.

She tried to get him to stop, saying his name again and again, but he continued to walk without taking any notice of her. He crossed the living room and went down the corridor to his bedroom. He flipped on the light, then stiffly gestured her to the chair by the window where she'd sat that first morning and waited for him to awaken. He placed the bouquet of red roses in her arms.

"Paul." She caught his sleeve as he tried to walk away from her. In the harsh overhead light, his features appeared to be formed in a mask of deadly calm. But his eyes were turbulent with hurt and anger.

He caught her hand and gently removed it, his expression never changing. "Please, Christy," he said quietly. "I have things to do."

He went to the closet, pulled out a dark blue garment bag, unsnapped the closure that folded it and opened it out on the bed. Chris's heart sank to the pit of her stomach.

A chilling acceptance settled over her.

"Who told you?" she asked flatly.

"Danny Tucker," he replied, going back to the closet and pulling out a fistful of shirts on hangers. He carried them back to the bed. "His wife had tossed him out and he was at the inn, consoling himself. Unfortunately—or fortunately, depending on whose point of view you take—he'd had too much consolation and happened to mention that he'd been asked to do a phony marriage license."

Paul spoke easily as he folded slacks over a hanger, then placed the shirts on top. He went back to the closet for shoes and placed them in the bottom of the bag.

"I wanted..." Chris's voice caught in her throat. She cleared it and tried again, making sure it was strong rather than desperate. "I wanted you to understand how much you'd hurt me. I wanted you to feel the same pain."

He zipped the bag closed, then looked up at her, his dark gaze focused on her like a laser sight. "Oh, I do," he said significantly. "Believe me, I do."

He walked to the bathroom and returned with his shaving kit. He turned the bag over and opened one of the pockets.

"Then I fell in love with you all over again," Chris said, the words torturing her as she spoke them. "And the whole scheme turned on me. I'm sorry."

"I imagine you are," he said, stowing the leather bag. "This isn't quite as good as getting me to show up at the church, all eager and lovesick, while you're heading in another direction on a 747. Do I understand the scheme?"

"Perfectly," she admitted. "That was the plan originally. But after a couple of days, life with you was everything I'd imagined it would be twelve years ago. And getting you to *want* to be married to me became the most important thing in my life."

He frowned as he went to the dresser. "And you expected deceiving me to accomplish that?"

She moved to the bed, flowers and all, and sat beside his bag. She dipped her head until he was forced to look away from the pocket of the bag and into her eyes. "It worked, didn't it?" she asked softly.

He straightened, placed his hands loosely on his hips and looked down at her with a calm she found completely unsettling. "Yes, it did. You made me regretful and desperate for you. You filled me with rosy dreams of a future filled with children and pets and a house on Beacon Hill."

"Sounds good to me," she said in a whisper.

"You *lied* to me," he reminded her brutally, his calm slipping.

"The morning I told you you were married to me," she said, "I lied. But after that—every kiss, every word, every lovemaking, was honest and from my heart. I love you, Paul."

He shook his head. "I don't believe that for a moment. If you've kept hate alive long enough to play this kind of trick on me, it couldn't possibly turn to love in a couple of weeks."

"You underestimate yourself."

He looked away with a scornful sound. "No, I don't. Any man stupid enough to think it's romantic to get a marriage license a second time and never once considers it could mean he'd never gotten the *first* one, deserves whatever he gets."

He folded the bag and snapped the closure. Chris placed a hand on the bag when he tried to lift it.

"Listen to me," she demanded. With an impatient sigh, he crossed his arms and shifted his weight to one leg. She stood and placed her hands lightly on his arms. "I'm telling you the truth, Paul. I love you."

"It's a little late for that now. I've already gotten the story from Danny."

"I was going to tell you when you came home." She looked into his eyes, trying to force her way past the shutters he'd closed against her.

"Christy—"

"It's true! I tried to tell you the night you made love to me, then I tried to tell you the following day, but things were still all mixed up for you with your father and—" She stopped, determined not to blame Louis.

He gave her a dark look. "After Danny told me I wasn't really married, I went to talk to my father again. He tried to cover for you, to tell me that he'd lured you into the scheme, that you wanted to tell me and he wouldn't let you. But I won't absolve you that easily. He may have conceived the plan, but you're the one who carried it out. You're the one who lay in my arms and whispered over and over that you loved me. You're the one I can't forgive."

Chris was certain he meant it.

She reached to the bed for the bouquet of roses. "Then why did you bring me flowers?" she asked quietly.

"Isn't that what you give an actress after a stellar performance?"

Paul saw the jab hit home. The pain in her eyes doubled, and her shoulders slumped. He had to look away, his own pain well beyond his tolerance level. He picked up his bag and turned to the door. He stopped there and turned to say without expression, "I've canceled everything—the chapel, the photographer, the flowers. I asked Carlotta to call everyone invited and explain that you backed out, deciding, after all, that I was a less than reliable risk."

He reached into the pocket of his jacket and placed two tickets on the dresser. "I didn't cancel the cruise tickets. I thought you might want to use them, anyway, with Erica or your mom."

Chris drew a deep, barbed breath. "So, here we are again. Three weddings that never happened for the same couple must be some kind of record."

He made a helpless gesture with his free hand. "Could be. Maybe we just weren't meant to love each other. 'Bye, Christy."

Chris heard his footsteps go through the house and out the door, and knew as surely as she knew her own

name that he was wrong. They *were* meant to love
each other. Would always love each other. She just
wasn't meant to *have* him.

Chapter Thirteen

"How *could* you?" Nate Bowman stopped pacing and came to stand over his daughter, who sat on a corner of the pink-and-green-flowered sofa.

His wife looked up at him, her expression pushing him back several inches. "She was in pain and wanted revenge," she said. "She's half yours, you know. Revenge is a concept I'm sure you understand. And added to the pain was the fact that she still loves him after what he did, and after all this time. She *thought* she was perpetrating a deception when subconsciously she was just being what she's always wanted to be—Paul Bertrand's wife."

"But she made him *believe* he'd married her. She let me climb all over him. She let everyone think—"

"Yes, she did," Jerina replied evenly. "Do you have a problem with that?"

"Of *course* I have a problem with it!"

"Then I don't want to hear it."

Nate stared at his wife as though she were extraterrestrial, then turned away to the kitchen. "I'll make another pot of coffee," he said faintly.

The moment her husband was out of the room, Jerina gathered Chris into her arms.

Chris sobbed shamelessly. She'd been a brick as she explained everything to her parents, taking full responsibility, but when her mother looked at her with the same unconditional love and understanding that had held her together twelve years ago, she fell apart. What kind of an idiot, she wondered about herself, could have messed up love twice with the same man?

"I don't know what to say, Chris." Jerina stroked her hair and patted her back. "Your course of action wasn't very wise, but love makes us crazy. It's just that...what you did to Paul is probably more than you can expect a man to forgive. And the timing was bad. Right after he'd just learned that his mother had been unfaithful to his father and had chosen to leave her child in order to keep her lover."

"I know." Chris sat up and dabbed at her eyes with a shredded tissue. That had all crossed her mind in the two hours since Paul had left. "I just wanted you to understand what happened. And to give you these." She handed her the cruise tickets.

"Chris, we don't want—"

Chris pushed them back at her mother as she tried to return them. "Please. It would make me very happy if you and Daddy took our places. Cruises are very romantic. At least..." Her throat tightened, but she swallowed and went on. "At least, that's what Paul says."

Jerina put an arm around Chris's shoulders. "Where is Paul now?"

"He...he left the Viper with Brent to cover the bet and took the bus to Boston. Jacqui came and told me."

Jerina squeezed her shoulders gently. "Maybe you should give it a day or two, then try to talk to him."

Chris shook her head, remembering very clearly the anger and disappointment in his face. "I don't think there'd be much point in that. He told me he'd never forgive me. I believe him."

"Well..." Jerina tried to speak bracingly, but her voice was strained with reaction to her daughter's pain. "You learned to live without him once before. And did very well."

Chris pulled her coat around her and stood. "Yes, I did." She'd been miserable, then resigned, then had found a comfortable if dreary way to go from day to day. But she hadn't slept with him in those days. She hadn't lived two weeks as his wife. She hadn't turned to him in the night and been taken in his arms.

"Why don't you stay here for a few days?" her mother suggested.

Chris shook her head and hugged her. "Thanks, but I'll be fine."

"Chris..." Jerina began to protest, but Chris was already out the door.

FRIDAY FELT to Chris as though it were six days long. It began with a telephone call from Erica asking for the day off.

"Of course you can have it off if you don't feel well," Chris said, "but I think I know what the problem is. Alex came to see me last night. I know about your asking him to take you to the woods."

"I know it was stupid," Erica admitted. "I was just desperate. I thought that might work when the wedding plans didn't. I guess you could say it was temporary insanity."

Chris laughed lightly. "He does love you, you know. That's why he did it."

"I know. I just need a day to kind of—you know—regroup."

"You sure?" Chris teased. "We were going to rearrange the shop today, remember? You sure you want to miss all that taking down and putting up again?"

"Oh, that's right." Erica sounded momentarily uncertain.

"Just teasing," Chris said quickly. There was no point in both of them being miserable and overworked. "Stay home. Regroup. And I'll see you Monday."

"Thanks, Chris."

She moved the entire front of the store to the back, then one side to the other. She put up a new display of shower invitations and changed the lingerie on the mannequin in the window from lavender lace to black silk.

When a group of giggling young women crowded into the shop, intent on a bridal-shower gift for a friend, Chris smiled and showed them around—and found forcing a cheerful demeanor one of the hardest things she'd ever done.

PAUL TURNED OFF the monitor on his computer terminal and fell back into his chair. He closed his eyes and tried to clear his mind. He achieved an instant of blankness, then Christy's face bloomed out of it as clearly as though she stood before him. He sat up and walked to the window. Boston spread out below him in frantic but picturesque splendor.

And right out there, on the steeple of a church, Christy's image stood in her blue, hooded coat, dark hair flying in the wind.

He studied it for a moment, remembering the morning she'd worn it when he'd walked her to work.

Then pain crowded the image aside and filled his being, taking over his world.

He didn't know why Christy's image haunted him. This was all her fault; she'd admitted it herself. *She* had tricked *him*. He had nothing to feel guilty about. His love had been honest.

He rubbed idly at the pain in his gut and found it curious that emptiness could hurt with such ferocity. He'd stared at the darkness most of the night, convinced he couldn't live without her. He kept imagining her softness against him, her hand on him, her hair on his shoulder, against his cheek.

By morning, pride had overridden the sense of loss. She'd tricked him. And he'd fallen for it.

A little corner of his mind was wondering if that was more the problem when he spotted Alex and Erica standing in the doorway of his office. For a minute, he thought his memories of Eternity had conjured them up. Then they walked into the office and Alex closed the door.

Erica approached him with a hesitant smile. "Can we talk to you, Mr. Bertrand?" she asked, reaching back for Alex as though she needed him for reassurance.

They wanted to talk to him about Chris. Why else would they have come all the way to Boston? But he didn't want to talk about her. He didn't want to remember that she'd made him believe she loved him as much as he loved her—and that it had all been part of a plot.

But they looked so fresh-faced and eager, and had obviously made the trip because they thought they could help. It wouldn't kill him to listen. And his anger at Chris was so deep nothing would change his mind, anyway.

"Sure." He pointed Erica to the chair next to his desk and pulled another one up for Alex. He sat on the edge of his desk and prepared to withstand their teenage views on love and romance.

Erica laced the tips of her fingers together and launched right into the subject. "I'm sure you know we came to talk about you and Chris." Before he could nod, she continued, "Well, I know it's none of my business, and Alex doesn't even think we should be here, but he didn't want me to drive into Boston by myself, even though I did better in driver's ed than he did. So he came with me." She spared her companion a look that combined exasperation with adoration. Paul smiled inside. But he felt too grim to smile outside.

Alex rolled his eyes. "Your parents have a better car for you to practice in than mine do."

Erica ignored him. "Yesterday, Alex and I weren't even speaking to each other, then Anita told me about what Chris did to you, and well . . . Chris is my absolute best friend, and all Alex does is talk about how he wants to be just like you when he's a reporter, so I thought we should try to do something. I want to tell you about Chris."

"Erica," Paul said patiently, "I know you mean well, but I know all about Chris. I've known her for a long time, too. And I just spent all that time with her, thinking—" He stopped, anger bubbling up in him all over again.

"Thinking you were married," she finished for him with detached efficiency. *She,* Paul thought, *would make a good reporter.* "I know. But she told me when I first found out you were married—or thought you were married—that she'd loved you since you were in high school and that she always knew you'd come back to be with her."

"She told me that, too," Paul said gently, "while she was lying to me about being married."

"But the part about loving you wasn't a lie. Because she told *me*. Maybe she'd lie to you, but why would she lie to me?"

Paul had to think that through. Meanwhile, Erica went on. "When Alex and I had that fight the morning we went to make an appointment at the chapel—" she waited for some acknowledgment that he remembered, and he nodded "—she told me that I shouldn't push Alex because I would drive him away, the way she drove you away. She said she'd always regretted it. And you know what else she did?"

He was already feeling overloaded. "What?"

"She gave Alex's parents enough money to send him to Boston College for a year, and she's going to try to get him the scholarship that the Eternity merchants give every year to someone in the community. Do you get it?"

Paul opened his mouth to tell her he did, but that it didn't—

"She's trying to fix with Alex and me what she messed up with you and her when you were young. I *know* she loves you. She doesn't look at any man the way she looks at you, and she seemed happier when she was married to you—or pretending to be—than I've ever seen her. Anita said so, too, and she's known her longer."

"Erica—"

"Just one more thing. She did something wrong." Erica paused and bobbed her head from side to side as though she didn't completely agree with that, but had to side with the majority. "But you did, too, when you left her. I mean, the first time. But she fell in love with you all over again. How do you know you won't fall in love with her again when you get over being angry?'' Erica came to a halt and took a deep breath. ''Well . . .''

She stood and offered her hand. ''Still friends?''

Paul took her small hand in his and shook it, his brain now like so much overcooked spaghetti. He couldn't think.

Alex lagged behind a moment as Erica headed for the door. ''The best thing about talking to Erica,'' he confided to Paul, ''is that all you have to do is listen.'' Then he asked hopefully, ''You coming home?''

Paul shook his head. ''Sorry, Alex. This goes a little deeper than you two can understand. But I appreciate your efforts.''

Alex sighed philosophically. ''We were afraid of that. So we brought along someone who understands these things better than we do.''

He nodded to Erica, who opened Paul's office door and admitted Louis. Alex and Erica stepped out into the city room and closed the door.

Paul turned away from Louis and went to the window, resentment tightening every muscle in his body.

''I told you I didn't want to see you,'' Paul reminded him stiffly, ''until I'd calmed down.''

''Well.'' He heard Louis's voice just behind his shoulder. ''I'm a performer. I'm used to flying in the face of danger. And I'm here because you're in more danger than I am.''

Paul glanced darkly over his shoulder. ''Don't be too sure.''

Louis ignored the implied threat. ''You're willing to risk your entire personal future because a young woman who deserved a little retribution made you realize you're vulnerable?"

Paul turned from the window, incensed that that was all his father thought it was. He jabbed his index finger into the shoulder of Louis's tweed jacket.

"You set me up between you!" he protested. "You wrote one of your little dinner-theater farces and gave me all the laughs. Well, I'm not amused."

"We had a point to make," Louis said calmly.

Paul's anger deepened. "That's what makes it all so reprehensible. You planned it! You set out to hurt me."

Louis shook his head. "I set out to make you see how much you need love—a woman's love—and *my* love."

"Really. Well, you blew it, Pop."

"Did I?" Louis followed Paul back to his desk, then stood beside it as Paul took his chair. "I don't think so. I think it worked. I think that's what all this anger is about. After your mother left, you put this black border around yourself and told me not to cross it. And you did the same with Chris. You walk away from anyone who makes love important to you."

"You *lied* to me!"

"Big deal! You've pretended I don't exist, and you left Chris like so much unclaimed freight."

"I was young and confused!"

"I was there to help you, if you'd only asked!"

Paul sank into his chair, too angry to trust himself to speak.

Louis braced himself with his cane and sat on the edge of the desk. "We took desperate measures to keep you close, she and I, to prove to you that you need us just as much as we need you."

"You baited a trap," Paul said wearily.

Louis nodded. "After waiting twelve years for you to come on your own, it seemed fair. She loves you, son." His voice became quiet and urgent. Paul resisted its effect. "I explained last night that she wanted to tell you sooner, but I wouldn't let her. I suspected you'd react this way. Then when we talked about your mother, I thought you finally seemed to have acquired a little understanding. Tell me I wasn't wrong."

Paul remained silent.

Louis leaned on the cane to get to his feet. He sighed and shook his head. "You know, Paul, in your work, you have a whole world before you. But in your heart, you've boxed yourself into a four-by-four cell. Goodbye."

When the door closed behind his father, Paul fell back in his chair, feeling as though he'd been run over by a train. When he could collect his thoughts again, he gave the kids credit for trying. But he found it hard to give his father credit for anything. He wouldn't even torture himself by focusing on Christy.

IT WAS HER WEDDING DAY. Rain drummed on the roof of Chris's apartment and beat against the windows, streaming in mournful streaks down the panes. She sat up in bed, thinking the sight was in perfect harmony with the stormy grief inside her.

Then she turned her mind immediately to all she planned to do at the shop today. She'd discovered during the night that she couldn't think about Paul without crying. So she'd indulged herself on the condition that the morning would bring a new resolve to start life over again. But she was already finding it far more difficult the second time.

She made a pot of coffee and toasted an English muffin, but found she couldn't eat it. She tidied the apartment and left for the shop with a commuter mug in her hand.

The Powell chapel drew her as surely as though she *was* getting married that day. She decided that stopping at the chapel was foolish and determined to go on to the shop. She was already late, and Erica would be off today. But even as she berated herself for doing it, she turned onto the road that would take her to the Powell estate and the chapel.

She parked around the side and sat in the car, staring at the quaint granite building with its diamond-shaped windows. Her imagination placed a bright sun in the sky and peopled the still-green grass with friends and relatives dressed for a wedding. She saw herself in the dress that had hung in her closet at her parents' house for twelve years, and Paul in a morning coat and cravat.

The pain the vision caused her was curiously comfortable. It helped expiate her stupidity somehow. She glanced at her watch. Nine fifty-five. Five minutes before the ceremony would have begun. Twenty minutes before she would have become Mrs. Paul Bertrand.

Chris got out of the car, walked up the stone steps and pulled open the old oak doors. The smell of polished wooden pews and flowers left from a previous wedding met her nostrils, and an all-pervasive quiet beat loudly against her ears.

Her imagination filled it with the sound of vows being exchanged. She went to the first pew and sat down, letting herself absorb what might have been— since this was all she would ever have of it.

PAUL RACED along the highway in a rented car, a speeding ticket already on the seat beside him. His lead foot on the accelerator flirted with another, but he didn't care. He had to get to Christy. He had to tell her he'd been a jerk, that he hadn't closed his eyes since he'd walked out on her, that he couldn't live without her—not even for the thirty-eight hours they'd been apart.

Last night Erica and Alex's pleas on her behalf had played over and over in his mind. And his father's patriarchal preaching finally forced him to take a good look at himself.

Christy had fallen in love with him again. He'd known her love was genuine when he'd left, just as he'd known the first time. But he'd been afraid, just like before. The world knew him as a savvy, worldly-wise journalist who saw inside every conflict and understood it—except the one within himself. The one that made it so hard for him to accept that he could love anyone when his mother had abandoned him without a second thought. It was hard to believe he was that vulnerable.

His hands opened and closed on the steering wheel as he longed for Christy with a desperation he'd never known for anything or anyone. He sped past the old lace factory, the bank, the bridge, and glanced down the side street for a glimpse of her car in front of her shop. It wasn't there. Maybe she'd taken the day off.

He glanced at the clock on the dashboard—10:10. He knew suddenly, certainly where she was. He did a U-turn on First Street, then roared off in the direction of the Powell estate. He pulled into the lot beside her car, tires screeching on the wet pavement, and leapt out of the car, heading for the back door.

CHRISTY WENT OUT the chapel's front door, holding it open with her shoulder, smiling through her tears as

e imagined herself and Paul greeting friends, shak-
g hands, looking lovingly into each other's eyes.

She would follow them to Mexico, she thought. She
pped out of the fantasy for an instant and looked at
e autumn-hued woods.

Mexico. The notion blossomed with appeal. She let
e door close.

AUL BURST THROUGH the back door of the chapel,
s heart thumping, his eyes scanning the solemn
hitewashed emptiness. He stopped a few steps in-
de and frowned, his disappointment overwhelming.
'here was she?

Then the movement from the front door caught his
e. He glanced to the front of the chapel and had a
impse of dark blue as the door inched closed.

He opened his mouth to shout, but no sound came.
'ould she want to see him? Would she forgive him for
hat he'd done to her—again? Doubt paralyzed his
ocal cords.

"Christy!"

Christy heard the shout behind her and turned in
me to see Paul running toward her down the chap-
's middle aisle. Then the door closed on the image.

She stared at the carved wood, wondering if she'd
agined that, if the picture existed only in her mind.
ut the sound of her name in that urgent shout lin-
red on the air, and her heart was thumping.

Then the door pushed outward and Paul stood
ere, looking very real. His eyes were alive with love
d anxiety, a pulse ticked in his jaw, and his hands
me up to close over her arms. Their touch bit
rough the sleeves of her coat as reassuring proof that
e was not a figment of her imagination.

He pulled her back into the church and let the doo close behind them.

"You *have* to marry me," he said, his voice as firr as his grip. "I'm sorry I walked out. It was injure pride, hurt feelings, stupidity. I know you love me.' He tightened his grip and demanded in a whispe "Please tell me you love me—that I'm not just kid ding myself because I love *you* so much."

"Oh, Paul." Chris felt her whole being empty o grief and regret and fill up again with hope. "I lov you. I've always loved you."

The admission weakened him and he slackened hi grip. She wrapped her arms around him and wept. H held her to him fiercely, strength returning as he fel the desperation and the need with which she held him

She drew back, eyes brimming with tears. "I'n sorry I agreed to the prank. At first I was being vengeful, but then it became so right, so precisely wha I'd always wanted, that there were times when I for got it wasn't real. I truly was going to tell you...."

He drew her back into his arms. "I know. It's a right. That part wasn't your fault but my father's."

She drew away again, refusing to let Louis take th blame. "No. It was his idea, but I'm the one who im plemented it with such credibility."

He nodded and framed her face, then leaned dow to kiss her forehead. "He did it because he knew you' turn in just such a performance—and that it woul cease to be a performance. He manipulated both of u because he knew we still loved each other."

That did explain many things. "That's downrigh Machiavellian," she said.

Paul laughed softly. "I think he did it so skillfull he might have even recoined the word. From now on brilliant subterfuge will be called Bertrandian."

"How did you know I was here?" she asked.

Paul put an arm around her and walked her toward the front pew. "Because I know you."

"I was pretending the wedding was taking place," she admitted with a wry twist of her lips. "As a sort of self-inflicted punishment for hurting you."

"We'll set it up again," he said, stopping her in front of the simple pulpit where Bronwyn married all couples who wanted their love to last forever. "As soon as we can get a date. Do you want to fly in the face of the odds and plan yet a fourth wedding?"

Chris closed her eyes and stood on tiptoe to kiss his lips. "I just want to be married to you, I don't care how many tries it takes."

"I don't believe a fourth wedding date will be necessary."

Bronwyn's voice broke the chapel's silence. Paul and Chris turned to find her walking out from the small anteroom where she dressed for services. She wore a charcoal-colored linen suit she often wore in her capacity as Justice of the Peace. She gave them an affectionate smile. "Why don't we just proceed with this one?"

They stared at her in surprise. Then Chris turned to Paul. "I thought you canceled everything?"

"I did," he assured her, then said to Bronwyn, "Remember? I spoke to you personally."

Bronwyn nodded. "But some things can't be canceled. Love is one of them. It doesn't matter how many times you turn away from it, *real* love is forever." She smiled again. "Why do you think we're called Eternity? It's more than our Indian name, it's our creed. We had a feeling you two would find a way to keep this date."

Paul raised an eyebrow. Chris frowned questioningly. "We?"

The back door opened, admitting Nate and Jerina, and Louis and Carlotta—dressed for a wedding, just as Chris had imagined them a few moments ago.

Chris's parents embraced her. Louis came to shake Paul's hand.

"We've been waiting in the museum," Jerina said. "All of us."

The front doors opened, admitting a stream of guests bearing gifts and wedding-day smiles. Jerina placed a garment bag over Chris's arm. It contained the wedding dress in which she'd just imagined herself. "Let's take this into the dressing room," she said, tugging at her hand, "and get this wedding under way."

Louis handed Paul a plastic bag emblazoned with the name Ted's Tuxedos and a duffel. "I *didn't* cancel the morning coats like you asked. I had a feeling we'd need them, after all."

Paul and Chris turned to look at each other over their shoulders as they were led off in opposite directions, friends slipping into pews, the buzz of low conversation swelling as the little chapel filled.

Their shared glance expressed amazement and, as the distance between them lengthened, acknowledged the absolute rightness of the wedding that would finally erase that distance forever.

CHRIS DRIFTED up the aisle on Nathaniel's arm, preceded by Anita in a pale pink dress that had also been purchased twelve years before. Erica wore a creative concoction of darker pink that included boots, a floaty skirt and a felt hat with one side of the brim turned up.

Chris experienced a sense of unreality curiously allied with the most crystal-clear joy she'd ever known.

The church fell silent, except for the ceremonial strains of June Powell's organ music.

Paul waited at the altar, Louis and Alex beside him. He watched Christy come to him with a radiant smile undimmed by the veil covering her face. He had to resist an impulse to stride down the aisle and meet her halfway to be certain that nothing diverted her, even now.

But she met his gaze and held it, promising without words that nothing would ever keep them apart again.

At the front of the chapel, Nate tucked Chris's arm into Paul's and gave him a reluctant smile of acceptance.

Handkerchiefs were already fluttering.

Bronwyn smiled at them as they stood before her. Then she glanced up at her congregation and smiled again. "Dearly Beloved, we are gathered here in the presence of God and this community to unite this man and this woman—*finally*—in the state of holy matrimony."

There was a spattering of laughter and the sound of quiet sobbing. Nate put an arm around Jerina.

The familiar words were spoken, the old questions asked and answered. Paul and Chris turned to one another, tied forever, though Bronwyn had yet to say the words. Paul was warmed by the joy in Chris's eyes, and she felt steadied by the love and possession in his. They reached for each other as Bronwyn's voice carried to the last pew in the chapel.

"Paul and Christine, I now pronounce you husband and wife—for all eternity."

SILHOUETTE

⟩SPECIAL EDITION⟨

COMING NEXT MONTH

SEPARATED SISTERS Kaitlyn Gorton

According to Clay Franklin, Ariadne Palmer had a twin sister! It was unbelievable! She couldn't deny his proof or her intense attraction to him, but she couldn't trust him either...for that meant accepting that her whole life had been a lie.

ASHLEY'S REBEL Sherryl Woods

That Special Woman! and *The Bridal Path*

Dillon Ford had always been wild and sexy, but now that Ashley Wilde had returned to her home town, she found the rogue even more intriguing. Did she dare to tame him and make him hers for keeps?

MARRY ME IN AMARILLO Celeste Hamilton

Gray Nolan would do anything to stop his sister's wedding, and he hoped bridal consultant Kathryn Seeger would be on his side. But Kathryn had no intention of changing his sister's mind about marriage, and every intention of changing his...

WAITING FOR NICK Nora Roberts

A Stanislaski story worth waiting for. Frederica Kimball felt like she'd been waiting her whole life to become a woman...waiting for the day when Nick LeBeck would fall for her. Now she's all grown up and the waiting is over!

MONTANA LOVERS Jackie Merritt

Made in Montana

Widowed mum Candace Fanon couldn't stop thinking about sexy stranger Burke Mallory, but she knew he wasn't telling the whole truth about why he came to town. Burke knew he could seduce Candace, but would she ever forgive him for lying?

DADDY OF THE HOUSE Diana Whitney

Parenthood

Bethany Murdock never imagined her ex-husband, Jay, could have the domestic touch. But when the tough cop broke his ankle and had to stay home and play house with his kids, it was the beginning of a wonderful reunion.

COMING NEXT MONTH FROM
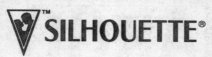 SILHOUETTE®

Intrigue
Danger, deception and desire

HERO FOR HIRE Laura Kenner
FOR YOUR EYES ONLY Rebecca York
FEVER RISING Maggie Ferguson
THE DEFENDANT Gay Cameron

Desire
Provocative, sensual love stories for the woman of today

THE FIVE-MINUTE BRIDE Leanne Banks
HAVE BRIDE, NEED GROOM Maureen Child
WEDDING FEVER Susan Crosby
A BABY FOR MUMMY Sara Orwig
TEXAS MOON Joan Elliott Pickart
MYSTERY MAN Diana Palmer

Sensation
A thrilling mix of passion, adventure and drama

HIDING JESSICA Alicia Scott
RENEGADE'S REDEMPTION Lindsay Longford
SURRENDER IN SILK Susan Mallery
THE LADY IN RED Linda Turner

MARGOT DALTON

first Impression

Be *very* careful who you trust.

A child is missing and the only witness tells a chilling story of what he's 'seen'. Jackie Kaminsky has three choices. Dismiss the man as a handsome nutcase. Arrest him as the only suspect. Or believe him.

"Detective Jackie Kaminsky leads a cast of finely drawn characters... An engrossing read."
—*Publishers Weekly*

"Jackie Kaminsky is a great addition to the growing list of fictional detectives."
—*Romantic Times*

AVAILABLE IN PAPERBACK FROM AUGUST 1997

FREE!

FOUR FREE
specially selected
Special Edition™ novels
<u>PLUS</u> a Mystery Gift
when you return this page...

Return this coupon and we'll send you 4 Silhouette Special Edition® novels and a mystery gift absolutely FREE! We'll even pay the postage and packing for you.

We're making you this offer to introduce you to the benefits of the Reader Service™– FREE home delivery of brand-new Silhouette novels, at least a month before they are available in the shops, FREE gifts and a monthly Newsletter packed with information, competitions, author pages and lots more...

Accepting these FREE books and gift places you under no obligation to buy, you may cancel at any time, even after receiving just your free shipment. Simply complete the coupon below and send it to:

THE READER SERVICE, FREEPOST, CROYDON, SURREY, CR9 3WZ.

EIRE READERS PLEASE SEND COUPON TO: P.O. BOX 4546, DUBLIN 24.

NO STAMP NEEDED

Yes, please send me 4 free Special Edition novels and a mystery gift. I understand that unless you hear from me, I will receive 6 superb new titles every month for just £2.40* each, postage and packing free. I am under no obligation to purchase any books and I may cancel or suspend my subscription at any time, but the free books and gift will be mine to keep in any case. (I am over 18 years of age)

E7YE

Ms/Mrs/Miss/Mr _____
BLOCK CAPS PLEASE

Address _____

_____

_____ Postcode _____

LINDA HOWARD

ALMOST FOREVER

THEY PLAYED BY THEIR OWN RULES...

She didn't let any man close enough.

He didn't lrt anything get in the way of his job. But Max Conroy needed information, so he set out to seduce Claire Westbrook.

BUT RULES WERE MEANT TO BE BROKEN...

Now it was a more than a game of winners and losers. Now they were playing for the highest stakes of all.

AVAILABLE IN PAPERBACK FROM AUGUST 1997